BONNIE AND CLYDE

A NOVEL BY BURT HIRSCHFELD

Based on the Screenplay by
DAVID NEWMAN & ROBERT BENTON

HODDER PAPERBACKS

Copyright © 1967 by Warner Bros. - 7 Arts Production

First published by Lancer Books, Inc.
New York 1967
Hodder Paperback edition 1967
Second Impression 1968
Third Impression 1968
Fourth Impression 1968
Fifth Impression 1968

SBN 340 04453 5

Printed in Great Britain for
Hodder Paperbacks Ltd, St. Paul's House,
Warwick Lane, London, EC4 by
Hazell Watson & Viney Ltd, Aylesbury, Bucks

Clyde was the leader, Bonnie wrote poetry.

C. W. was a Myrna Loy fan who had a bluebird tattooed on his chest. Buck told corny jokes and carried a Kodak. Blanche was a preacher's daughter who kept her fingers in her ears during the gunfights. They played checkers and photographed each other incessantly. On Sunday nights they listened to Eddy Cantor on the radio. All in all, they killed 18 people.

They were the strangest damned gang you ever heard of.

This is what the reviewers had to say about the film:

THE GUARDIAN
. . . Bonnie and Clyde belongs with the best of them

EVENING STANDARD
It cries out to be seen

NEWS OF THE WORLD
. . . exciting, disturbing and damnably clever

THE OBSERVER
. . . simply stunning

THE TIMES
Don't miss it

SUNDAY MIRROR
. . . stunningly fresh

DAILY MIRROR
Sizzling entertainment

DAILY SKETCH
. . . bitter often painfully funny . . .

THE TIMES were hard. The great depression lay across the land and suffering spread and many lives were shattered. Factories closed down. Businesses failed. Men were thrown out of work and despaired of ever finding jobs. Small farms were possessed by banks and farmers were ordered off the soil. War veterans peddled nickel apples on the streets of the cities and took nourishment at soup kitchens. Politicians, well fed and addicted to platitudes, foretold a corner around which prosperity waited. Few people ever turned that corner.

Anger and bitterness intensified. Dry-eyed women could do nothing to ease the hunger of their children or the torment of their husbands. Families piled their belongings into old cars and headed west; others split up, never to be reunited, and young men frequently went out on their own, taking what they could find out of life. It was 1932 and the times were hard.

In the states of the Southwest the land baked under a hot, white sun, all existence slowed, the juice of life running slow. In West Dallas, Texas, the air was thick and oppressive, an infectious stillness that stretched to the horizon and put Bonnie Parker in mind of the mournful cadence of a funeral as it headed for the cemetery outside of town.

West Dallas was a place dying without hope and Bonnie Parker wanted to scream out in protest. It wasn't fair. She was young and good-looking and her brain and body craved excitement and adventure. Somewhere outside of her mother's old frame house, beyond West Dallas, beyond Texas itself, perhaps, there existed a world rich and full of rewards for a girl with her gifts. How? she asked herself. How could she find that world, become a part of it? There had to be a way.

Her pale blue eyes raked swiftly over the small, second-story bedroom. There was a shabbiness about it, a shabbiness she had sought to disguise with new curtains and a collection of porcelain figurines. She sighed, patted a bead of perspiration from her upper lip, and gazed at herself in the full-length mirror.

The naked image she saw in the glass pleased her. Her body was properly round but satisfyingly lean, the skin smooth and taut. Her breasts were high and glowing and no girl drew more admiring glances from the young men in town. And some of the older ones, too, the ones who had wives. A slow smile turned the corners of her rosebud painted mouth; she appreciated young men, their strong arms and flat bellies. Appreciated them a lot.

Resentment flooded her middle and she pivoted away from the mirror. *Damn* the men of West Dallas, dull, soft with surrender, accepting without protest the hand fate dealt them. She could marry any one of them, bear him a litter of squawling brats, and become old before her time. Become a duplicate of her own mother, weary and dried out, never smiling, never knowing any fun, finding no pleasure in life.

Not for Bonnie Parker!

She heaved herself onto the bed and pounded the comforter with her fists. There had to be a better life. Something different, exciting, rewarding. She rolled onto her back, breasts slightly flattened, ribs cording the pale skin, her belly a gentle rise. Narrowly she eyed the painted bedstead, so like a cage. She struck it with her fist. Again, harder. Harder still. A sharp pain stabbed through her hand and she sat up, swearing softly at the brass bars. Somehow, she told herself. Somehow she would find a way and get out. Out of this dingy house, out of West Dallas, out of this empty life. Still naked, she moved purposelessly across the room and stood at the window, looking out.

Everything was the same. The same deep sky, cloudless and hot, the same empty street, dusty and still, the same dirty white wooden houses. At first she didn't notice the man in the dark suit as he strolled up to her mother's car, parked in the driveway below. When she did see him she was unimpressed. His clothes owned no special style, the padded shoulders too wide, the jacket sacklike, the trousers baggy and dusty. A wide-brimmed Panama hat shadowed his face.

What would he think, she wondered, if he were to look up and see her standing jaybird naked in the window? That would give him a thrill, something to tell his buddies about.

She frowned. What was he doing around her mother's car? She watched him peer through the open window at the dashboard and at once remembered that the keys were in the ignition. A flash of apprehension slithered through her middle.

The man straightened up and glanced in both directions, and in that microsecond she knew that he planned to steal the old car. He reached for the door handle and Bonnie filled her lungs with air.

"Hey, boy!" she called. "What you doin' with my mama's automobile?"

His head swiveled around and he looked up, squinting against the glare. He was younger than she had imagined, about her own age or a year older. No more than twenty-two for sure. There was something in his face, an intensity, a recklessness etched into the crinkles around his eyes, in the set of his mouth. She watched the first flush of fear wash away, replaced by an expression of delight at what he saw.

Let him look, she thought, an impudent half-smile angling

7

across her full mouth. Give him a good look. A knowing smile spread his lips and at once she enjoyed his seeing her this way, naked, and she knew that there was something special about him, some private element in him that was also in her that made it possible for her to understand him, to know what was in his brain almost as soon as he did. Her grin broke open.

"Hey, boy!" she called. "You wait there, hear!"

She dashed across the small room to her closet, shoved her feet into a pair of shoes, and draped a white dress over herself, buttoning it as she hurried down the stairs.

He was waiting in the street. An arm's length away, she stopped short, staring at him. He stared back.

"Ain't you ashamed?" she challenged provocatively. "Tryin' to steal an old lady's automobile?"

He grinned happily. "I been thinkin' about buyin' me one."

"Bull," she laughed. "You ain't got money for dinner, let alone to buy no car."

He shrugged exaggeratedly. "Now, I got enough money for Cokes," he said, "and since it don't look like you're gonna invite me inside ..."

"You'd steal the dinin'-room table if I did."

He took a step down the street. 'Come to town with me then. How'd that be?"

"Goin' to work anyway," she said after a beat, falling into step beside him.

"Goin' to work, huh? What do you do?"

"None of your business."

He frowned as if thinking hard. "I bet you're a ... movin'-picture star. No ... a lady mechanic? ... No ... a maid ..."

"What do you think I am?" she blurted out, flaring briefly.

"A waitress," he said quietly.

"Well, yes," she said, wondering how he knew. "What

8

line of work are you in? When you're not stealin' cars."

"I tell you," he said mysteriously. "I am lookin' for suitable employment right at this moment."

"What did you do before?"

He let the words out with contrived casualness, "I was in state prison."

"State *prison!*"

"Yeah."

"Guess some little old lady wasn't so nice." she said mockingly.

He stared at her coldly. "It was armed robbery."

They were in town now, on the main street, between facing rows of flat-fronted shops and stores and a couple of cafés. Except for themselves, the street was deserted. A scraggly dog shuffled across the street, tail tucked between his legs.

"What do y'all do for a good time around here," he said, "listen to the grass grow?"

"Guess you had a lot more fun up at state prison?"

He laughed and pointed to his right foot. "See this foot? I chopped two toes off of it with an ax."

"Why?"

"To get off the damn work detail, that's why. Want to see?"

"No!"

They began walking again, not speaking. After a while, Bonnie said, "Boy, did you really do that?"

"Yeah."

"You must be crazy."

At the gas station on the corner, he bought each of them a Coke. They leaned against the soft-drink cooler and sucked on the bottles, letting the fizzy liquid cut the dust in their throats. She watched as he removed the Panama hat and rolled the cold bottle across his forehead. She *did* like his face, and the quick, uncertain way he grinned.

9

"What's it like?" she said almost shyly.

"Prison?"

"No, armed robbery."

He shrugged. "It isn't like anything."

She considered that. It sounded wrong to her, as if he were making it up, trying to impress her. Annoyance crept into her voice. "Hah! I knew you never robbed noplace, you faker."

He stared down into her eyes and she felt something else. The cold strength of him, a threat as if he might *do* something. Do *anything*. A shiver rode down her spine.

A quick movement, reaching under his jacket, and when his hand reappeared there was a .38 revolver in it, glinting blackly in the sunlight. There was a special quality to *this* gun in *his* hand and she touched it with the tips of her fingers, gently, lovingly, stroking softly. She wet her mouth and looked up at him.

"Yeah," she murmured. "Well, you got one all right, I guess. But you wouldn't have the gumption to use it."

He searched the street, settling on the grocery store across the way. "You just keep your eyes open." He strode up onto the wooden sidewalk and disappeared inside the store, never looking back.

Bonnie waited, a new excitement pounding along her nerves, a thickness in her throat, a sick-making anticipation in her middle. It was difficult to breathe.

He backed slowly out of the store after a couple of minutes, the revolver in one hand, a fistful of money in the other. Halfway across the street he looked at Bonnie and smiled and she couldn't help but smile back, pleased and warmed by his presence, charged by him and what he had done, She yearned to launch herself at him, to roll in the dusty street with him to feel his strong arms around her, to taste his mouth.

Suddenly the grocer appeared on the sidewalk, shouting for help. Bonnie saw the young man in the Panama hat raise the pistol and an icy chill took hold of her. A shot crashed out and the bullet smashed into the sign above the store. The grocer retreated out of sight.

Bonnie's new friend watched him go, laughing; then he turned and held out his hand to her. Together they ran down the street to the edge of town. A car was parked in the shade of the last building. A gesture sent Bonnie into the front seat while he swiftly and efficiently lifted the hood and found the proper wires to cross.

"Hey!" she called. "What's your name, anyway?"

The wires joined, he slammed down the hood. "Clyde Barrow." He got in beside her and started the car, racing the motor.

"I'm Bonnie Parker," she shouted, in order to be heard. "Pleased to meet you."

Clyde grinned and gunned the car into motion, accelerating swiftly to ninety, speeding them on their way. Together.

2

SHE COULDN'T wait. The excitement stabbed deep into her bowels and she was all flesh and desire and only he could fulfill the strange dark cravings she felt.

She was all over him, mouth working fiercly across his flesh, onto his ear, his neck, hands reaching under his shirt, feeling the tight flesh of his belly, moving lower. He twisted and squirmed under her, fighting to control the car, foot heavy on the accelerator.

She grabbed for the steering wheel and yanked hard, sending the car off the road among some trees. He hit the brake and the car jolted to a stop.

She was at him again, unintelligible sounds rasping back in her throat as she plunged herself atop him, forcing him backward, reaching, searching, straining to find and take what he alone owned for her.

"You," she got out. "You ready?"

"Wait ..."

"Aren't you ready? Well, get ready."

She fumbled with his clothes. "C'mon, honey. C'mon, boy ... let's go ... let's ..."

"Hey! Hey, wait . . . quit that now, cut it out. I said, *cut it out!*"

He shoved her away, abruptly and painfully, slamming her against the far door. She glared at him, fighting for breath, saw him adjusting his trousers. He climbed out of the car.

What happened? she asked herself silently. What went wrong? The way she felt! It couldn't have happened if he hadn't felt that way too. She fumbled in her purse, found a cigarette, hunted desperately for a match. Clyde leaned through the open window and extended a light.

"Look," he said with forced casualness. "I don't do *that*. It's not that I can't, it's just that I don't see no percentage in it. I mean, there's nothin' *wrong* with me. I don't like boys," he ended defiantly.

"Boy," Bonnie said, trying to pick out her thoughts. Her brain was a whirling sump and she wasn't certain of what she felt; rejection, disgust—both, perhaps, and a great deal of fascination. She'd never met anyone like Clyde Barrow. "Boy," she repeated. "Boy, boy, boy . . ."

"Boy, what?"

"Your advertising is dandy. Folks'd just never guess you don't have a thing to sell." She hesitated. "You better take me home now."

He slid behind the wheel and closed the car door. "Wait." He reached for her.

She jumped out of the car. "Don't touch me!"

"If all you want's a stud service," he shouted after her, "then get on back to West Dallas and stay there for the rest of your life." She stopped running and listened as the words poured out with almost evangelical fervor. "You're worth more'n that, a lot more, and you know it, and that's why you come along with me. You could find a lover boy on every corner in town and it doesn't make a damn to them whether you're waitin' tables or pickin' cotton, so long as you co-operate. But it does make a damn to me."

She turned to face him. "Why?"

"Because you're different. You're like me and you want different things." She took a step back toward the car and the words came out of him faster now, more intense. "You and me travelin' together, we could cut clean across this state, and Kansas, too, maybe dip into Oklahoma, and Missouri or whatnot, and catch ourselves highpockets and a high-heeled ol' time. We can be somethin' we could never be alone. I'll show you ... when we walk into the Adolphus Hotel in San Antone, you wearin' a silk dress, they'll be waitin' on you and believe me, sugar, they're gonna know your last name."

Again that craving was upon Bonnie, now stronger, more intense, crazily swinging, a weird dark tempo beating in her chest. "When'd you figure that all out?" she said huskily.

"First time I saw you."

"How come?"

"Cause you may be the best damn girl in Texas."

She stared at him. "Who are you, anyway?" she said softly.

He opened the car door. "Get in."

She did.

They drove in silence until they came to a roadside café. Once inside, and settled in a booth, Clyde began to talk about himself, not for long, but enough so that she understood who he was and where his roots found nourishment.

He had been born in 1909 in Telco, Texas, another mouth to feed in a large family of poor sharecroppers. Just folks. He had begun stealing in his teens and it was while robbing a filling station that he was caught. It meant the penitentiary for two years, to be released for good behavior. Finished, he pointed a finger at her.

"*I'll* tell you about you," he said.

"I'll bet," she challenged.

The grin came and went. "Lessee ... You were born somewhere around East Texas ... got a big ol' family, right? ... You went to school, o' course, but you didn't take to it much 'cause you was a lot smarter than everybody else

14

anyway. So you just quit. Now ..." His brow ridged as if he were deep in thought. "When you were sixteen ... no, make it seventeen, there was a guy who worked in ... the ... uh ..."

"Cement plant," she put in quickly.

"Right. Cement plant. And you liked him 'cause he thought you was just as nice as you could be. You almost married that guy, but then you thought, no, you didn't think you would. So you got yourself a job in the café. And every mornin' you wake up and you hate it. You just hate it. And you get down there and you put on your white uniform ..."

"Pink."

"And the truck drivers come in to eat greasy burgers and they kid you and you kid them back, but they're stupid and dumb, boys with big tattoos all over 'em, and you don't like it. And they ask you for dates and sometimes you go, but mostly don't, and all they ever try is to get into your pants whether you want it or not ... and you go home and sit in your room and think, *when* and *how* will I ever get away from this?"

And *now*, she told herself silently, measuring him closely. Now she knew how and when. Clyde Barrow was the answer and the time was now. *Now*.

The waitress came over with their food. Clyde looked up at her, gaudy with makeup, spit curls plastered to each side of her forehead. His gaze went back to Bonnie, to her golden spitcurls. He said nothing until the waitress was gone. Then, pointing at the curls, "Change that. I don't like it."

She nodded once, reached for her hand mirror, and brushed the curls back into her hair. Clyde nodded approval and she smiled and began to eat ravenously.

"God," Clyde said. "You're a knockout."

Dusk was settling over the countryside when they emerged from the café. Bonnie followed Clyde toward the car they had stolen. He walked past it to a newer, more colorful model, a greenish-yellow sports coupé.

"Hey," Bonnie said, pointing. "This is the one we came in."

"Don't mean we have to go home in it."

Bonnie woke alone and frightened. For a long terrifying moment she didn't know where she was. Then it all came flooding back. The night before she and Clyde had come across an abandoned farmhouse and decided to sleep there. She glanced around the room. No Clyde. Where was he?

"Clyde . . ." She came to her feet, panic welling up in her throat. "Clyde . . ."

"Hey, lady."

She swung back, to see his grinning face peering in at her through a broken window. There was a pistol in his right hand.

"Where you been keeping yourself?" she said, ashamed of her fear and still gripped by it.

"Slept out in the car," Clyde replied casually.

"Oh. These accommodations ain't deluxe enough for you?"

There was that quick grin and she felt reassured. "If they're after us," he said, "I want the first shot. Come on, you got some work to do."

She joined him outside. On the dilapidated picket fence that ringed the house, six old bottles had been propped up. Without a word Clyde turned and rapidly fired six shots. The bottles exploded, one after another.

"Say, you're good," Bonnie said.

"The best."

"And modest, too."

"Come on," he said. "Got you all set up over here." She trailed after him around to the side of the house where an old automobile tire was suspended on a rope from the limb of a big oak tree. He handed the gun to her and indicated the tire. "Set her spinnin'," he said.

Bonnie nodded. She extended her right hand, bracing it with her left.

"Uhuh. One hand."

She set her lips determinedly and obeyed. She pulled the trigger. The shot went wild and the kick of the revolver sent her reeling backward.

"That's all right," Clyde said. "Again. Come down slow with it . . ." He demonstrated, bringing his empty hand down as if aiming, leveling off, clicking off an imaginary shot. "Now you."

Bonnie followed his instructions, squeezed off a shot. This time the tire whirled around as the slug tore into it.

"Ain't you somethin'!" Clyde exulted.

Grinning happily, Bonnie blew smoke from the barrel in exaggerated self-mockery.

"I tell you," he went on, "I'm goin' to get you a Smith and Wesson, it'll be easier in your hand. All right, now. Try it once again . . ."

Bonnie sighted on the tire, raised the revolver, and brought it to bear. At that moment a man appeared behind them.

"Howdo," he said.

Snatching the pistol out of Bonnie's hand, Clyde whirled, sighting on the man's middle, ready to shoot.

"*No* sir," the man said, suddenly full of fear. "No sir. Now y'all go right ahead with what you're doin'. Just go right ahead."

Clyde eyed him warily assessing. The soiled shirt and wide-brimmed hat, the worn overalls, the weatherbeaten face. A farmer.

"Used to be my place," the farmer said. Clyde straightened up and lowered his weapon. "Not any more. Bank took it."

The farmer moved off toward the front of the building, Clyde and Bonnie close behind. There was a decrepit Ford parked on the road, bulging with household belongings. A woman with a baby sat in the front seat and a small boy stood alongside the front fender.

"My folks," the farmer explained. "Yes sir, the bank moved us off. Now it belongs to them." He pointed and Bonnie and Clyde followed the gesture. A foreclosure sign had been nailed onto the front door of the farmhouse. It read,

PROPERTY OF MIDLOTHIAN CITIZENS BANK
TRESPASSERS WILL BE PROSECUTED

"Well, now," Bonnie said, "that's a pitiful shame."

Clyde shook his head sympathetically. It was happening all over, back home in Telco, in Oklahoma, New Mexico, Iowa, banks taking over from the small farmers, putting them out as if they were less than livestock. Not the proper thing to do to folks. He began to load his revolver.

"You're damned right about that, ma'am," the farmer said to Bonnie.

From behind the Ford, another man appeared, an old Negro, and he stood some distance away waiting.

"Me and him," the farmer said. "Me and him put in the years here. Yes sir. So you all go right ahead. We just come by for a last look."

For a brief interval the farmer stared at the farmhouse, then turned and shuffled toward his family. Clyde and Bonnie watched him go. A growing anger rose in Clyde, a deep urgency to strike out, to inflict pain. He whirled and pulled three times at the trigger. Three slugs tore into the foreclosure sign.

The farmer looked back.

Clyde offered the gun. The farmer looked at it and almost smiled. He hefted the pistol in his hand, slowly brought it to bear. He fired and hit the sign. He glanced over at Bonnie and Clyde, who smiled their approval.

"Y'all mind?" he said. "Hey, Davis," he called to the old Negro. "Come on over here."

Davis came closer and Bonnie took the second gun from

Clyde and gave it to him. Davis looked at Bonnie, at the farmer, and finally at the house. The farmer turned and snapped off another shot. A window shattered. He nodded and Davis raised the gun he held and aimed carefully before firing. Another window crashed into shards. Davis's seamed face broke into a pleased grin as he returned the weapon to Clyde, nodding his thanks.

"Much obliged," the farmer said. He offered Clyde his hand and they shook. "Otis Harrison's my name. And this here's Davis."

Clyde acknowledged the introductions. "This is Miss Bonnie Parker and I'm Clyde Barrow." He hesitated, an idea leaping vividly to life in his frontal lobes, the excitement of discovery throbbing in his chest. It was *right*, perfect, and he rolled it around his brain joyfully. "We rob banks," he added.

3

THEY TALKED about it a lot during the rest of the day and into the night. Both of them felt the same surging desire, the same awareness that this was for them, that this was what they wanted, that this was right. Right in every way.

"Where is the money nowadays?" Clyde asked.

"In the banks," Bonnie answered, giggling with anticipation.

"Right. And that money truly belongs to the ordinary folks, folks like us, right?"

"Right."

"And the banks go 'round foreclosin' on people like Mr. Harrison and Davis, and that ain't fit."

"Not a bit."

"If a man's goin' to make a livin' these days he's just naturally got to go where the money is."

"That's right, Clyde."

"And it's in the banks."

The logic was unassailable and all that was left was to choose their first target and do it. Just do it. They would simply walk in and wave those revolvers around a little and take some money and skeedaddle out of there. Nobody would be hurt. Not one single solitary soul. They were very firm about that.

"No shooting," Bonnie said a number of times.

"Hell, no," Clyde agreed. "Won't be no need to. Nobody's fool enough to kick up a fuss about money belongin' to a bank, so it'll all be peaceable and friendly like."

There was one more problem to be settled. "It'll be fun," Bonnie said, "scaring people and taking the money. I'm just hankerin' to see the expressions on the faces of them bankers when we come walkin' in on them . . ."

Clyde stared at her stiffly. "*We* ain't walkin' in on nobody. Least not this first time. I am goin' to do this by myself."

"But why?"

"Because I say so is why. And because somebody's got to stay in the car so's we can make a fast getaway. Right?"

Bonnie could not argue with that and said so. When she went to sleep finally her disappointment was tinged with anticipation for the experience the new day would bring. They slept in each other's arms like two children, brother and sister, innocent and untroubled.

Clyde had selected the town to be hit, and the bank. He had seen it once and recalled thinking that it would be an easy job. The bank was on a corner with little automobile traffic, which would make for a swift escape after the job. All that was needed was a single determined man with good nerves. And Clyde Barrow was such a man.

By midmorning they were on the road. Bonnie drove, Clyde beside her, hat pulled low over his eyes, hunched forward, staring at the long ribbon of road ahead.

"You just stay in the car and watch and be ready," he said, certain that Bonnie was frightened, thinking to strengthen her resolve.

Bonnie gripped the wheel tightly, knuckles white, her face set and tense.

"Right," he said. "Okay, now," he went on, trying to

remember how Jimmy Cagney had done it in a picture he had seen. He took a gun from the glove compartment and put it on the seat next to Bonnie. "You just be ready if I need you," he said, voice flat and meaningful.

"I'll be ready."

They drove without saying anything for a while.

"Scared?" Clyde asked.

"Me?" she said quickly. "No, not me."

They drove on.

"Say," Clyde said, breaking the silence. "What are you thinkin' about?"

"Nothin'."

"Oh."

Bonnie slowed the car at the outskirts of the town, negotiating carefully. The bank appeared.

"There," Clyde said. "There's the bank."

"I see it."

She eased the car up to the curb in front of the bank and braked to a stop. Neither of them spoke for a moment. Bonnie worked her hands over the wheel. She glanced over at Clyde.

There was no mistaking the stiffness on his face, the tightness of his mouth, the glazed look in his eyes. He was frozen in his seat, as terrified as she was.

"Well," she managed. "What are you waitin' for?"

One short glance and Clyde was out of the car, hurling himself at the bank entrance. Inside, gun in hand, he allowed a beat or two for his eyes to become adjusted, to pick out the lone teller in his cage. The man seemed drowsy, half-asleep over his ledgers. And there were no customers.

It was all wrong, but there was no time for Clyde to think, to sort the jumble of impressions that crowded his brain. He strode aggressively toward the teller, gun outstretched. Once again Clyde conjured up an image of Cagney, glared at the man in the window, turned his lip in a snarl and growled out the words.

"This is a stickup. Just take it easy and nothin' will happen to you. Gimme the money."

The teller raised his head lazily. There was no apprehension on his face and his voice, when he spoke, was easy and conversational. He almost smiled.

"Howdo."

"Gimme the money!" Clyde snapped.

This time the teller did smile. "What money? There ain't no money here, mister."

Clyde swallowed. What did this mean? His eyes raked the empty cages, again noting the absence of customers, the abandoned executive desks. "What do you mean there ain't no money?" he said, voice growing shrill. "This here's a bank, ain't it?"

"This was a bank," the teller said. "We failed three weeks ago."

"What? What?" A rising panic gripped Clyde. What would Bonnie think? She'd mark him down as a failure, a man who couldn't finish what he started, whose nerve went when the going got rough. She would never believe this story unless she heard it for herself. He should have brought her along. Perhaps he should get her, let her talk to the teller herself. There was no time for that. Rage began to build in him. He ducked behind the dividing partition and grabbed the teller by his shirt front, then twisted him around and shoved him towards the front, gun prodding his back roughly.

"Move, dammit man. Move." The words came from between gritted teeth. "Outside."

Bonnie saw them and stiffened with fear. What did this mean? What had happened to make Clyde bring back a hostage? Nothing had been said about taking captives. She saw the anger on Clyde's face, the dark, smoldering look in his blue eyes. He jabbed the stranger with his gun, sent him tripping toward the car.

"Tell her!" Clyde commanded. "Tell her!"

The man blinked, eyes darting nervously, certain he was

in the hands of a pair of lunatics. "As I was tellin' this gentleman, ma'am our bank failed last month and ain't no money in it. I sure am sorry about that."

The fear drained out of Bonnie at once and almost hysterical relief took its place. It was funny, all of it, two country folks making like bank robbers and ending up with a bank that was flat busted just like themselves. She began to laugh. Louder and louder.

Clyde glared at her, his anger mushrooming, a torrid, frustrating thing. With one swift motion, he knocked the teller to the ground and dived into the car. Bonnie released the brake, still laughing. Clyde wanted to strike out with words, with his fists. He thrust his gun arm out the window, aiming at the bank window with its gilt legend—ASSETS: $70,000. Four shots rang out and a small hole appeared in each of the zeros. Seconds later the entire window came crashing down.

The car roared off across the plain, Bonnie Parker still laughing.

4

BONNIE COULDN'T stop laughing for long. Every time she managed to quell the laughter the scene outside the bank came back to her, the sight of Clyde angry and brandishing his pistol, herding that frightened little bank clerk in front of him, a bank clerk with no bank, with no money. It *was* funny. A giggle sputtered across her lips.

"Go ahead," Clyde said thinly, his anger close to the surface. "Laugh more."

"I can't help it, hon."

"We got $1.98 and you're laughin'. I ain't laughin.' There's nothin' funny from where I sit."

She tried to stop and succeeded for a while. The car sped along the road past mile after flat mile of empty fields, of burned-out corn fields, past deserted farms, through villages that seemed uninhabited. Now, as they went through one town. Clyde checked the main street. There was no one in sight. Up ahead a grocery store came into view.

"Pull up," he said brusquely.

"What for?" Bonnie asked.

His eyes were cold when he spoke. "Pull over, I said, and keep the motor running."

She did and watched nervously as he climbed out of the car. She had never seen him in this mood before and it troubled her. Like this, he was capable of anything. She wished she hadn't laughed at him. Well, not really *at* him. Just at the way their first bank holdup had come so undone, nothing about it right. She exhaled softly. Maybe Clyde wasn't cut out for this kind of work. Maybe both of them weren't. She glanced at the grocery store. What was taking so long?

When Clyde entered the grocery, he had eyes only for the clerk. He failed to see the butcher in the back of the store.

"Afternoon, mister," the clerk said. "What'll it be?"

"A loaf of bread, I reckon, and a dozen eggs."

"Yes sir." He fetched the order. "Anything else?"

"Some butter, I guess, and some sliced ham and some sausages. And some vegetables and canned fruit, too." The clerk assembled the items and bagged them, toting up the cost. He punched open the cash register and looked up, smiling, about to ask Clyde for the money. The smile froze on his face as he saw the black revolver gleaming in Clyde's hands.

"This is a stickup, mister," Clyde said. "I'll take all the money in that cash drawer."

The clerk hesitated and Clyde reached across the counter, grabbing for the bills. He came up with a handful and grinned happily at the immobilized clerk. This was more like it. Easy pickings.

Clyde never saw the butcher, huge and thick-bodied, coming at him with catlike silence, brandishing a meat cleaver. The cleaver came slicing through the air, barely missing Clyde, lodging in the wooden counter. Clyde leaped backward, protesting.

"Hey, I don't mean to hurt anybody!"

The butcher moved with incredible swiftness for a man of his size and bulk, enveloping Clyde in a bear hug around the chest, pinioning his arms, lifting him off the ground.

Fear was a living thing in Clyde's gut and he struggled to free himself, to loosen his gun hand. The butcher fought fiercely, making thick grunting noises, ignoring Clyde's protests that he meant no harm, bearing him over backward. They crashed to the floor and the breath whooshed out of Clyde. He gathered all his strength for one last attempt to free himself. No use. The butcher tightened his grip. They rolled over and Clyde tried to raise the barrel of his pistol to an upward angle. His strength and determination were fast draining away and he grew terrified at the thought of capture, of being returned to prison.

He braced himself against the floor and forced his arm loose and swung hard at the butcher. It did little good. The butcher fought harder. The two men went tumbling across the floor, knocking over a display of canned goods, sending a standing shelf to the floor, breaking bottles.

"Let go!" Clyde cried hysterically, struggling wildly. Momentarily he broke away, only to trip and go to the floor, the butcher on him at once. The great arms tightened until Clyde feared his chest would burst.

Summoning all his strength, Clyde staggered erect, carrying the other man with him, striking out with pistol. He felt the butt crash against the other's face, heard the soft squish of bone and gristle, saw blood spurt out of his forehead. Clyde broke for the door, the butcher hanging on desperately.

Both of them went tumbling onto the sidewalk. Frantic now, Clyde struck out hard, pistol-whipping the butcher, turning his big fleshy face into a crimson pulp. For a long interval nothing happened; then the strength went out of the big man's hands and he slumped to the ground. Clyde tore away, shouting at Bonnie as he ran for the car.

"Get the hell out of here! Get the hell out of here!"

Bonnie stepped down hard and the car leaped ahead. A moment later they were tearing off across the flatlands again.

"What happened?" she said.

"I didn't want to hurt him." Clyde gasped. "I didn't. It was only money. Why'd he have to get in it? Why? It was only some money."

27

Bonnie concentrated on her driving.

"Damn him, the big son of a bitch. He tried to kill me. I ain't got no eyes in back of my head. What he want to do a fool thing like that for?"

Bonnie fought the wheel as they made a curve on two wheels, rubber screeching.

"A man tryin' to get a little food around here and some dumb son of a bitch tries to kill him. It wasn't even a real robbery. Just some food and a little bit of dough. I'm not against him. Didn't he know that? I'm no different than him, just folks. I might've killed him and I didn't want to kill no one. I'm not against him. I'm not."

He looked over at Bonnie as if expecting her to speak, but she made no reply.

"Damn," he said. "Damn dumb son of a bitch."

After a while, Clyde lapsed into a brooding silence that went unbroken as they sped across the seemingly unchanging landscape. Once he dozed and his head sagged forward, only to jerk upright. He glanced sidelong at Bonnie as if fearing some criticism, wary of sleep as he might have been wary of an enemy. It was the sound of the engine that snapped him back to full alertness. It began to cough.

"What's that!" he muttered.

"What?" Bonnie said.

"The motor. Listen. There. There it is again. There's something the matter with the damn thing."

She listened and frowned. "I didn't hear nothin'."

The hoarse sound came again and quickly repeated and the car bucked and bucked again before continuing ahead. The motor continued to give voice to its affliction and there was intermittent bucking in counterpoint.

"You see! You see!" Clyde said excitedly, focused entirely on this mechanical problem, and grateful for the diversion. "There is somethin' the matter."

"Can you fix it?"

He glared at her as if about to speak, then fell back in the seat, expression mournful. "We better find us a good garage someplace. Keep a lookout."

Bonnie looked over at Clyde at frequent intervals. The last time he grinned at her and she understood that his usual good humour had returned. The misadventure in the grocery was behind him, almost forgotten and of little consequence. She returned his smile and turned her attention back to the road.

It was just a filling station at a crossroads, ramshackle and in need of a painting. There was no sign of life but as they rolled up a figure stepped out of the doorway of the tiny office, wiping his hands with a dirty rag. Bonnie stopped the car.

"Ain't goin' to be a mechanic here," Clyde complained. "Not in this ol' beat-up place."

"Maybe this fella can help. Or direct us to a first-rate garage." Bonnie was hopeful, but even her optimism paled at the sight of the man approaching. There was nothing about him to inspire confidence.

He was small, made up of a succession of round protrusions. His bottom was round as if in counterweight to his thrust of chest; and his face was cherubic, pink and glowing. His eyes were circular and large, unblinking and his nose was a red button. His mouth was a perfect bow. His dirty yellow hair was curly and thick and he had needed a haircut many months before.

"How do," he said in a high-pitched voice.

"There's somethin' wrong with the motor," Clyde said. He got out and stretched.

"What?" the little round man said.

Bonnie gave him one of her sunniest smiles. He was not very bright, she decided, but he was all they had and right now they needed his help.

"We thought you could tell us," she drawled softly. "And put it right too."

"Well, I don't know." He scratched his head. "What's been happenin'?"

Bonnie mentioned the coughing and the bucking.

He nodded and opened the hood of the car. "Turn on your engine, please, ma'am."

Bonnie did. The little round man listened with interest. A nervous smile came and went when the motor sputtered, missed, ran on uncertainly.

"You can turn off the engine now, please, ma'am."

Bonnie did so.

The little round man reached and they saw him disconnect the fuel line. He leaned forward, sucked air deeply into his lungs, blew hard into the fuel line. Clyde and Bonnie exchanged a look of dismay. This country boy wasn't going to be of any help, not this way, for sure.

The little man took another breath and blew again, his little round cheeks growing redder. For a moment Clyde was convinced he was going to inflate himself and float away and he was struck by the weirdness of the situation. A dull flat noise in the fuel line interrupted the thought. The mechanic straightened up and screwed the fuel line back into place, his round head gently bobbing up and down. He slammed the hood down and locked it.

"You can start up your engine now, ma'am," he said.

Bonnie did and exclaimed delightedly as it purred smoothly.

Clyde slapped his hands together. "Hey, what was wrong, anyway?" he asked.

The other man shuffled his feet shyly. "Air bubble—clogged up the fuel line."

Clyde moved around the car so that the mechanic stood between himself and Bonnie. He stared down at the smaller man. "Air bubble," he repeated softly.

"That's right." The mechanic looked from one to the other with uncertainty. He ducked his head. "I just blowed her away, you see."

A pleased but disbelieving grin broke across Clyde's face. "You just blowed it away."

The mechanic nodded and belched. An embarrassed blush spread across his cheeks. "Scuse me, ma'am." He looked from under his brows at Clyde. "Anythin' else I can do for you folks right now?"

Clyde looked across the top of the round yellow head to where Bonnie sat in the car. He jerked his head vigorously. Bonnie got the message and directed her attention back to the mechanic.

"Well, now," she murmured, smiling softly. "I am not sure. . ." She let her eyes ride with no particular hurry around the premises. "Say," she went on. "The little red things there, stickin' up? Are they gas pumps?"

The mechanic followed her eyes. "Sure," he said soberly.

"Isn't that interestin'?" She turned her most brilliant smile on him. "How does that there gasoline get in my little ol' car?"

The mechanic stepped forward, anxious to be helpful. He gestured toward the pumps. "Well, ma'am, y'see, there's this tank under the ground, and the gas comes up this tube into the pump and into your car, ma'am."

"My, my," Bonnie said throatily. "You are surely a smart fellow. I mean, you sure do know a lot about automobiles don't you?"

The round man nodded vigorously in assent. "Yeah," he said proudly. "I reckon I do."

"That's a fine thing," Bonnie said.

"Yes, it is," Clyde put in. "A fine thing. A man could go far if'n he owned a talent for automobiles like you have."

"Well, now," Bonnie said. "Would you know what kind of a car this is?"

The mechanic considered the question. A pleased smile turned the bow mouth and he patted the hood of the car. "Yes, ma'am. This is a Chevrolet 8-cylinder coupé."

Bonnie shook her head. "No, it isn't."

That drew a quick worried frown. "Sure it is."

Bonnie leaned forward, eyes fastened to the mechanic.

31

"No," she said with no special emphasis, "this is a *stolen* Chevrolet 8-cylinder coupé."

The mechanic's hand leaped off the hood as if it had suddenly been scorched by the devil's inferno.

Clyde took a single step forward and the smaller man stepped back, eyeing his two customers warily, curiosity and fear alternating on his features. He wiped his hands on his greasy blue Levis and ducked his head. The round eyes blinked and looked away, came quickly back to Bonnie, to Clyde, trying to perceive if he was being mocked. He kicked dust and stared at a pebble he had never before seen.

"You ain't scared, are you?" Clyde said.

The little man shrugged and didn't seem to know what to do with his hands. "No, I ain't scared."

"I believe he is scared," Clyde said to Bonnie.

"What a pity," she said.

"Shoot," the mechanic muttered, not looking up.

"We sure could use a smart boy who knows a lot about automobiles," Clyde said to no one in particular.

"You a good driver, boy?" Bonnie said.

"I guess so."

Clyde measured him. "No, I don't think so. He's better off here where it's quiet and there ain't no trouble."

"What's your name, boy?" Bonnie asked quietly.

"C. W. Moss."

"What's the C. W. for?"

"Clarence Wallace."

Bonnie nodded gravely. "I'm Miss Bonnie Parker and this is Mr. Clyde Barrow." She paused and almost smiled. "We . . . rob . . . banks."

C. W.'s little round eyes widened and a nervous laugh trickled across his lips.

"Ain't nothin' wrong with that," Clyde said, making his voice hard. "Is there, boy?"

"Uh, nope . . ."

32

Bonnie gave an exaggerated sigh. "No, I reckon he ain't the one."

"Unless, boy," Clyde said, "you think you got enough guts for our line of work?"

C. W. felt a twinge of resentment. These two, with their big talk questioning his courage, his nerve. A man might be only a back-country filling-station mechanic but that didn't mean he didn't know his way around, hadn't done things. "Look here," he said, displaying his displeasure. "I served a year in the reform school."

"A man with a record!" Bonnie said.

Clyde laughed, a scornful sound, full of doubt and insult, a sound that penetrated to some dark, vulnerable place in C. W. "Now look," Clyde said. "I know you got the nerve to short-change old ladies who come in for gas, but what I'm askin' you is have you got what it takes to pull bank jobs with us?"

"Mr. C. W. Moss?" Bonnie added.

C. W.'s eyes went from her to Clyde and back again. "Sure I could," he said hurriedly, anxious to gain favour with this beautiful girl, the most beautiful girl he had ever seen. "Sure I could. I ain't scared, if that's what you think."

"Prove it," Clyde said without expression.

They watched him carefully. There was the fleeting smile, the uncertain lowering of his eyes, the toe of his boot scratching earth, and a quick turn. He walked back inside the office and they saw him open the cash drawer and reach in, to come out with a handful of bills. Seconds later he was back outside, face giving no indication of his thoughts. He walked up to the car, thrust his hand at Bonnie, and dropped the money in her lap.

Clyde let out a long rising whoop of pleasure, pulled open the rumble seat of the coupé, and helped C. W. climb in.

They drove off, laughing, all three of them.

5

THE DAYS and nights passed swiftly and unmarked as they spent most of their time driving along back roads or in dingy rooms in motor courts. The three of them slept in the same room and at first it was fun and comfortable, sort of family like, until Bonnie began to grow tense. It wasn't that she didn't like C. W.—she did. She *did*. A lot. But his snoring kept her awake and besides she wanted to be alone with Clyde, to be able to do those things a real woman did with a man, to a man, to make him want her the way she wanted him.

She couldn't understand *that* about Clyde, about his not craving her, her *body* in the same way all the boys did back in West Dallas. She remembered how it was when she was waiting tables in that truck stop, all those big old rough boys coming in and funning with her, laughing all the time, their eyes saying what it was they wanted, what it was she had for them, and some of them said it with their hands and with words. And sometimes. . .

But it was Clyde now, only Clyde. She loved him fiercely and desired him more than she had ever desired anyone or anything. To look at him evoked longings in her she had never before known and she ached, *ached*, to be filled with.

him, to give him everything that was hers to give. It was important, she told herself, that they be alone, that they begin to live in a natural way for a man and a woman. She would talk to Clyde, explain how she felt, and he would understand. C. W. would simply have to sleep by himself.

Her chance came sooner than she expected, the next day when they stopped off in a roadside café for lunch. The three of them were seated in a booth in the rear, Clyde able to watch the door from his position. But he and Bonnie were concentrating on C. W. instead.

The little round man was industriously preparing his food. With methodical thoroughness he sprinkled sugar over everything, spreading a thick layer of the white granules over the beets, the potatoes, the meat. Bonnie could remain silent no longer.

"C. W., what are you doin'? Why do you do that?"

C. W. put the sugar shaker aside and began to eat. "Why not?" he said.

"It's just disgusting, that's why."

C. W. chewed with great relish. "Not to me it ain't."

Bonnie grimaced. "But . . . but it makes everything *sweet!*"

C. W. grinned up at her. "Yeah, I know."

Bonnie leaned back in her seat, an expression of despair on her face.

"Oh, damn!" C. W. exclaimed.

"What's wrong?" Clyde said.

"No mayonnaise."

C. W. slid out of the booth and went down to the far end of the counter. Bonnie waited until he was beyond hearing before speaking.

"Clyde," she said, "why does he have to stay in the same room with us?"

It was as if Clyde failed to hear the question. His face remained concentrated, his eyes narrowed in thought. He reached for the sugar shaker, spread a thin field of white on the dark surface of the table, and began to sketch a design in the sugar.

"Lemme show you about tomorrow," he said.

"Why?"

His brow ridged in tight focus. "Now, C. W.'ll be waitin' right outside in the car. Here is the teller's cage, four of them, and over here the desks and what have you. . ."

"Why, Clyde?" she persisted.

"What?"

"In the same room with us?"

He looked up, face dark. "Hell, where else? Ain't goin' to spread out all over the state." Clyde was startled by the harshness in his own voice and he arranged a slow, warm smile on his mobile mouth, going on more softly. "Not about to spread out, not yet, anyway. Now." he went on, turning back to the plan etched in sugar, "the door to the bank is here. You cover me from there."

She took his hand and lifted it to her cheek, cuddled her face against his palm. "It's just that I love you so much, Clyde."

"You're the best damn girl in Texas," he murmured, meaning it.

Just then C. W. returned, a jar of mayonnaise clutched in one fist. He looked down at the table in dismay. "Hey, you spilled all the sugar."

Clyde began to eat. "This is the layout for tomorrow up in Mineola."

"Mineola!" C. W. said, sliding into the booth. "Gosh, that's four, five hundred miles from here!"

"So what! We take U.S. 85 to Willis Point and cut over on State Highway 28 at Kaufman, keep on goin' till we hit the farm-to-market road that connects to 105 and that's right up by Mineola. On a Saturday afternoon. . ."

They listened closely as he told them how it was going to be.

Mineola might have been any one of a hundred similar

towns in the state of Kansas in the year 1932. On a sunny Saturday afternoon, the streets were crowded with cars and horse-drawn wagons, with families in town to shop for the week. People were talking about the political posters that were beginning to go up around town, photographs of President Herbert Hoover and there were even some of that Democrat Roosevelt; no Easterner with a funny way of talking was going to get many votes in Kansas, that was for sure, people said.

No one paid much attention to the big touring car that rolled down the street and stopped in front of the bank. Nor did anyone take notice of the young couple who got out, no different from the folks living around Mineola.

Clyde bent and looked through the window at C. W., who was behind the wheel. "Keep it running and be ready to go."

"Yeah, Clyde." C. W. smiled.

Bonnie and Clyde moved off toward the entrance of the bank, a nondescript brown wooden building with offices on the floor above.

C. W. didn't watch them. He was too busy looking for a convenient parking space. There, exactly what he wanted. A car parked halfway up the street behind him and pulled out. C. W. shifted into reverse and gunned the touring car back. He eyed the space and decided that it was just large enough to accommodate his car. It was a tight fit, but he maneuvered skillfully until he was in place. Once parked, he leaned back, satisfied with his effect, eyes glued to the bank entrance, waiting for Bonnie and Clyde to appear.

Inside the bank, matters were proceeding smoothly. When Bonnie and Clyde appeared they saw that only one guard was on duty, a scrawny little man whose best years were behind him. Clyde very calmly shoved his pistol in to the guard's face and relieved him of his weapon.

"All right, folks," Bonnie announced in a friendly voice, "this is a holdup so put up your hands, please, and do as you're told."

Arms shot skyward and eyes widened and one woman dropped her purse in fright and another uttered a small muffled shriek. The lady tellers were speedily accommodating, shoving stacks of bills through their grills so that Bonnie could fill the sack she carried.

"That's it, Clyde," she announced finally.

"Right." He smiled. "Now you folks just stay calm and quiet while we leave. Once we get out of town, why, you can make all the fuss you like."

He motioned for Bonnie to precede him, then ducked after her into the street. Squinting in the bright sun, they ran for the spot where they had left C. W. and the touring car. Neither driver nor car was in sight.

"What the hell. . . !" Clyde broke out. "Where's the car?"

Bonnie's eyes darted about anxiously. "There! Down the street!"

"Let's go!" Clyde shouted to C. W. "Let's go!"

C. W. slammed the car into gear, twisted the wheel, and struggled to shoot out of the parking space. There wasn't room enough. He slipped into reverse, backed fast, turned hard on the wheel, and shot forward again. He was jammed in tight. Back and forth he went now, banging bumpers with the car in front and the one in back, struggling frantically to wheel the touring car out into the roadway.

"Come on!" Clyde bellowed, waving frantically, looking back over his shoulder at the bank, expecting armed pursuit at any moment. "Come on! Get it out!" He gestured to Bonnie and they broke for the car and dived into the back seat even as C. W. struggled to free himself from the parking space.

"Come on!" Clyde cried. "Get it out of here! Let's get movin' before the police show up!"

C. W. swung the wheel hard and bore down on the accelerator. The big car lurched forward and there was the sound of scraping fenders.

A policeman came running up to the bank and the guard

pointed to the car up the street. The blue-clad officer went for his gun, began shooting.

"Get out of here!" Clyde screamed.

The car swung into the middle of the street and careered wildly, C. W. fighting for control. As they came alongside the bank, a dignified, white-haired man in his shirtsleeves and a celluloid collar leaped onto the running board, pounding at the closed window. Clyde recognized him as one of the bank officials.

"Stop!" the man cried. "Stop this car!"

"Get off!" Clyde shouted. "Get off before you get hurt."

"Oh, my God," Bonnie gasped. "Clyde, do something."

"Get away!" he shouted, voice crackling. He brandished his pistol. "Get off!"

The man pounded at the glass with his fist and in punctuation a shot whizzed overhead. From behind came the wail of a police siren. They were being followed.

It was too much for Clyde. The oppressive sound swelling inside his skull, the rising excitement and terror, the distorted face on the other side of that glass, so close and threatening recalling another face from deep in his past, another threat. A thin scream of despair broke out of Clyde and he turned his pistol on the man and fired.

An exploding sunburst of glass and the face turned into a horrible bloody mask. For an endless moment it hung there, a disembodied apparition, terrifying, the end of life, the violent visage of death. The face disappeared and Clyde fell back, moaning.

Behind the wheel, C. W. fought a continuing battle with the car and with his nerves. He hadn't expected anything like this. And it was all his fault, putting the car into that too-small space. What had he been thinking about? He glanced up at the rear-view mirror. A police car was careering after them, red flashes marking gunshots. All at once none of it was fun, none of it glamorous or exciting. But there was no time for such thoughts. Not now. Now was the time to escape, to elude their pursuers, to find some sanctuary. Somewhere.

They had no more than a few minute's lead over the police as they raced through the town. It was Bonnie who saw it first, realized that this was their chance to escape.

"Turn off, C. W.!" she cried. "At the next corner."

He did and Bonnie led the way out of the car.

"Come on. Follow me."

Without question, they accepted her authority, hurrying back around the corner to the moving-picture theater in the middle of the block. The marquee read, GOLDDIGGERS OF 1933.

"We're goin' inside," Bonnie said. "They'll never think to look for us here."

"Shoot," C. W. mumbled. "I seen this picture."

They found seats in the rear of the orchestra, Bonnie on the aisle, C. W. one seat away, Clyde in the row behind. C. W. scrounged down and attacked the candy bar he had purchased from the vendor in the lobby.

"We're lucky," he announced in a hoarse whisper. "It just started. You ain't missed much."

Bonnie focused on the black-and-white shadows on the screen, a row of dancing girls in white shorts on a lush set, tapping their way up and down a curved staircase. And Ginger Rogers was singing, "We're in the Money." Bonnie hummed along with her.

"I just love musicals," she tossed over her shoulder at Clyde.

He shook his head nervously, his eyes drawn back to the entrance doors. He felt for his pistol, jammed down in his belt. If anything happened . . . He changed his position and glared at the back of C. W.'s head.

"Boy," he said, voice tight with rage. "Boy, you gotta be poor in the head. You know what you did?"

"I wasn't thinkin' right, Clyde."

"You almost got us all killed, you know that? Killed."

C. W. turned and smiled what he hoped was a winning smile. "That bank man was the only one that got killed, Clyde. You sure did him good."

"You. . . !" Clyde struggled to keep his voice down. "Count of you I killed a man. Murder . . . you too."

"I'm sorry, Clyde."

"Dumb ass stupid."

C. W. turned again, nodded in full agreement. "Dumb ass stupid, that's right."

Clyde lifted his hand as if to strike him, slapped limply at the back of C. W.'s head. "Ever do a dumb thing like that again, and I'll kill you, boy!"

C. W. directed his attention back to the screen, smiling softly. The candy was nice and sweet and the girls on the screen were very pretty.

"I mean it, boy," Clyde added.

"Hush up," Bonnie said to Clyde. "You boys want to talk why don't you go outside?"

6

THEY HAD gone out of their way to reach this particular motor court, and C. W. wondered about that. Generally they took a room at the first one they came to toward dusk. Not this time. This time Clyde had known exactly where he wanted to go, had brushed aside all objections.

Once they were situated, C. W. wondered some more why it had had to be this motor court. There was nothing special about it. Just a collection of nondescript cabins around a parking area. And the rooms were no different, the same unpainted walls, the same cheap furniture, the same hard beds. Of course, this one did have a radio, which he supposed was something. He wished Bonnie would change the station though. She was listening to Rudy Vallee and C. W. got nothing out of those romantic ballads sung in that kind of reedy voice. He preferred a good old country singer.

"How come we come to this place, Clyde?" he asked.

Clyde looked over at him and grinned. "Because I said so."

"Oh. But why?"

"Because I'm goin' to meet my big brother Buck here, is

why. He's on his way right now. I wrote and tol' him where I'd be at and said to come on along and say howdo. He's a great ol' boy, Buck is."

"Suppose he doesn't come?" C. W. said.

Clyde's face darkened. "Buck'll come. He'll come cause he's real folks."

Later that evening, while C. W. bathed himself, Clyde sat on the edge of the bed cleaning their guns. Broken down, each part was carefully wiped off, then a light coat of oil applied before the weapons were reassembled. Clyde ignored Bonnie's conversational attempts and she finally grew bored and went into the bathroom.

C. W. was sitting in a tub of gray soapy water, energetically scrubbing his back with intense concentration. Bonnie stood in front of the sink and studied her face in the mirror. Having reached a decision, she wiped off her lipstick and began to do her mouth over again, shaping it carefully. Finished, she tilted her head to one side, then the other, assessing her handiwork. She turned to face C. W., who was leaning against the sink, lighting a cigarette.

"Look at me, C. W.," she said gently.

He interrupted his ablutions. "Yeah?"

"Do you like it?"

"What? Like what?"

"My mouth."

He stared without blinking. "Sure. I guess so."

"I mean, the lipstick. I put it on differently. Not so much. Lighter and a different shape. See?"

"Oh. Sure, I see. It's very nice."

"What do you think of me, C. W.?" she asked idly.

"Uh . . . well, you're just fine, I guess. Uh . . . well, course you're a real good shot . . . and . . . uh . . . well, sometimes you look pretty as a painting."

Bonnie turned back to the mirror and studied her face again. Yes, she decided. It was true. She was very pretty. And this new way of making up helped a lot. She brushed at her

43

blonde hair, arranging it so that it fell softly behind her ears. There. That gave her a softer, more womanly appearance. She liked that.

"Hey, uh, Bonnie," C. W. said. "Could you get me that washrag there? Toss it over, please."

Automatically, she went to the towel rack and pulled the washcloth off. She took two steps toward the tub and was about to flip the cloth square to C. W., when she hesitated. A slow, insinuating smile lifted the corners of her mouth and her pale blue eyes narrowed. She held the washcloth out at arm's length, let it dangle teasingly.

"Whyn't you come get it?"

"Huh?"

Bonnie waved the washcloth the way a toreador waves his cape. C. W. stared at it fixedly.

"Whyn't you come get it, C. W.?"

He started to shove himself erect, then realized that to do so would expose his nakedness to her. He blushed and fell back in the water.

"Aw, Bonnie," he said lamely. "Come on, gimme it, willya please?"

"Here it is," she taunted. "All you got to do is come get it. Ain't you got the strength to climb out of that there bathtub, C. W.?"

"It ain't that. . . ."

"Then what?"

He ducked his head. "Shoot," he mumbled. "You know."

She grinned. Slowly, very slowly, one leg reaching after the other, she moved closer to the tub, eyes fixed on him all the time.

"I'm goin' to bring it to you myself," she let out very quietly.

He saw her coming, saw that she meant to come close enough to stand over him, saw that the water offered no screen to his nakedness. He brought his knees up and tight together in a swift movement that sent waves breaking along the length of the tub.

"Aw, Bonnie, give it here."

"Sure, C. W. That's what I'm goin' to do."

She was within arm's length now and C. W. cast around frantically for something with which to shield himself. Nothing was available. In one quick motion, he reached out and yanked the washcloth from Bonnie's hand. The maneuver caused a great splash and Bonnie jumped back to keep from getting wet.

She stared at C. W., scrounged down in the tub like some gross sea creature afraid of the air, and wondered what in the world she could have had in mind. C. W. was not for her, a lump of a man, no challenge and no promise. His very presence was demeaning to her and to Clyde.

"You simpleton," she struck out harshly. "What would you do if we just pulled out some night while you were asleep? Did you ever think about that?"

C. W. stared up at her, eyes rheumy and soft with anguish. "Aw, I wouldn't know what to do. But you wouldn't do that, Bonnie. You couldn't, could you?"

Bonnie felt weary all at once, a weariness born of some indefinable inevitability about all this, about what C. W. had said, about her relationship with Clyde, about the way they were living. Where was the promise of that first day, of that moment when Clyde had robbed the grocery, of that wild, crazy ride afterward? Something was wrong and she yearned desperately to repair it. She looked down at the tub.

"That's right, C. W.," she said with resignation. "We'll always be around to take care of you."

She took a last drag on her cigarette and flipped it into the tub, unable to laugh as C. W. scrambled out of the way. She went back into the other room, slamming the door behind her.

Clyde was still perched on the bed laboring over his guns, mostly assembled and gleaming. There was an air of quiet preoccupation about him as if he had been thinking thoughts alien to him, reaching into deep areas of his being not often explored. He looked up as Bonnie entered.

"I want to talk to you," he said evenly. "Sit down."

She hesitated, stirred by this unfamiliar facet of his personality. She was used to a Clyde Barrow who was happy and laughing or alert and physical, ready to move to action, or an angry Clyde. But not this one. Not this quietly determined man. She lowered herself to the edge of the bed.

"This afternoon," he said, voice low as if reaching back into his memory and finding it painful. "This afternoon we killed a man and we were seen. Now nobody knows who you are yet, but they're goin' to be after me and anybody who's runnin' with me. Now that's murder now and it's goin' to get rough."

Bonnie chewed her lower lip and nodded but said nothing. After a beat, he went on.

"Look," he said haltingly, picking his words with care. "I can't get out, but right now you still can. You say the word and I'll put you on the bus to go back to your mama. 'Cause you mean a lot to me, honey, and I ain't goin' to make you run with me. So if you want, you say the word, hear?"

Tears formed in Bonnie's eyes and she tried to blink them away, seeing Clyde as a distant, wavering figure, distorted but oh, so beautiful. She shook her head stubbornly.

"Why?" he persisted. "Bonnie, we ain't goin' to have even a minute's peace."

Bonnie dried her eyes and tried to smile. She didn't like him this way, all glum and serious, making out as if the future held nothing but trouble and suffering for them. She knew better than that. Just knew it.

"Shoot," she said, placing a smile on her newly defined mouth. "Ain't you the gloomy thing!"

He took her hand and held it tightly. "Bonnie, you got to understand. We could get *killed*."

A laugh burst out of her. Death held no fear for Bonnie

46

Parker. Death was something folks talked about, something that happened to old people and sick people. To *other* people, not her. Not Clyde Barrow. Another laugh and she raised Clyde's hand to her cheek.

"Who'd wanna kill a sweet young thing like me?" she teased.

He smiled at her innocence, at her loveliness, at her failure to understand. She was the best damn girl in Texas. Absolutely the best.

"*I*," he pointed out with wry humor, "ain't no sweet young thing."

"Oh, Clyde, I can't picture you with a halo, and if you went to hell I reckon you'd rob the devil blind, so he'd kick you right on back to me."

The words conveyed to Clyde the depth of her feeling for him and he was moved by it. He leaned over and his mouth came down on hers, gentle, searching, unsure. Her arm circled his neck and he allowed her to draw him down on the bed. Her lips parted and her tongue danced wetly against his teeth. A rising passion flickered in his groin and a soft moan trickled out of him as he adjusted himself on top of her.

They rolled over. There was a hardness digging into her. She lifted her position, reached, and brushed a couple of guns to the floor. Her arm went back around him. Seconds later she was guiding his hand to her breasts.

Clyde found it difficult to breathe and his brain seemed to tilt and pitch inside his skull. A deep darkness enveloped him and it was as if he was tumbling through endless space, striving for some saving handhold and finding nothing. Down, down, down he went, toward some foreordained disaster.

He broke out of her embrace and heaved himself erect. There was a coarse thickness in his throat and his head was still spinning. His heart thumped irregularly in his chest and his hands were damp and hot. He moved to the window to stare unseeingly through the dirty glass.

Bonnie watched him, looking so beautiful in silhouette

against the window, kind of sad, lost, and almost ... holy. She loved him more that moment than ever before and wanted him in a way she had never wanted him before. She settled back down on the bed, her head resting on one of the guns. Slowly, she turned until her cheek pressed against the cold, hard barrel, her gaping lips against the muzzle. A spasm rode through her body and another and she waited for it to pass.

7

THE BLACK SEDAN bounced along the narrow dirt road past green slopes and brown fields. Its tires were worn and caked with mud and the body of the car was layered with dust, indicating that it had traveled far and over many unpaved country roads. A main highway appeared ahead and the driver straightened in his seat and squinted anxiously before allowing his jowled face to relax into a pleased grin.

"Won't be long now, Blanche. Not long atall."

The woman sitting beside him, the residue of a girlhood prettiness still on her face, made a small sound of assent and continued to study a well-worn copy of *Screenland* magazine. Vaguely one hand rose to finger the brown curls that had escaped from under her new hat, a close-fitting helmet of tan straw.

The man grinned and shook his head. He was feeling fine, *real* fine. And why not? Soon he'd be seeing his brother again, good ol' Clyde, and they'd have some great ol' times, the two of them. He glanced quickly, guiltily at the woman—the *three* of them. Blanche was his wife and he'd best be remembering that. He reached out and prodded the little fuzzy doll suspended from the rearview mirror by a shoestring and laughed back in his throat as it danced on its perch.

It didn't take much to make Buck Barrow happy. He was a big man, strong, inclined to fat, with a roll around his middle and the beginnings of a second chin. And anticipating the reunion with Clyde filled him with an immense joy. The Barrows had always had this strong sense of family, knowing that they belonged to each other, that no matter the distance between them they were irrevocably joined, part of the same flesh, the same blood.

A short happy laugh erupted out of Buck's fleshy mouth. He began to sing,

> "What a beautiful thought I am thinking
> Concernin' that great speckled bird,
> Remember his name is recorded on the pages
> of God's holy word. . ."

There was something about that hymn that moved Buck, that took him back to his childhood, that filled him with awe for the meaning of life—and death—that made him feel kind of strange and . . . *immortal*. He continued to sing.

"Buck," Blanche said, not looking up from her magazine. She had been reading a story, with pictures, about Ruby Keeler and how hard she worked to polish her dancing for the moving pictures so that everything she did would be perfect. Blanche admired that in a person, especially a woman, because she knew how difficult it was to be perfect, even if you did try all the time. She raised her head and looked at her new husband and smiled kindly. That was one of the things about being a churchgoing Christian—you learned to forgive people who weren't absolutely perfect. "Buck," she repeated, an almost nagging lilt in her voice.

He patted her knee. "What's that, my darling wife?"

"I want to talk to you."

He nodded vigorously but with no anticipation. Blanche,

he had already learned during the brief span of their wedded life, was a persistent woman with a strong sense of right and wrong and a pervading desire to keep their lives on the straight and narrow. Well, all right, Buck told himself silently. But Clyde was his brother, his blood kin, and they were just going to visit. Just visit.

"All right," Blanche said, her manner broadly coquettish. "Now you did foolish things as a young man, honeylove, but you went and paid your debt to society and that was right. But now you are just gettin' back in with the criminal element."

Buck frowned. "Criminal element! This is my *brother*, darlin'. Shoot, he ain't no more criminal that you are, Blanche."

"Well, that ain't what I heard."

Buck reached out to pat her knee but she moved and his hand came down on the ukelele that rested on the seat between them. He stroked it affectionately. "Now," he said, "word of mouth just don't go, darlin', you gotta have the facts. Shoot. Why, Clyde and me growed up together, slept and worked side by side." He laughed loudly at the recollection. "Goddammit, what a boy he was, full of ideas and always wantin' to do things."

"No need to use the Lord's name in vain, Buck-honey," she remonstrated.

"Sorry, darlin'."

After a minute, she spoke again, keeping her eyes fastened to the road ahead. "The thing is, Buck, your brother's a crook."

Buck filled his lungs with air. Two loyalties were in conflict within him: he loved Blanche, loved her dearly, but he also loved Clyde, and they'd been family a lot longer time. Why couldn't Blanche understand that?

"Now you stop bad-mouthin' Clyde, Blanche," he said chidingly, as if speaking to a child. "We're just gonna have us a little family visit for a few weeks and then we'll go back to Dallas and I'll get me a job somewheres." He hesitated and his voice firmed up. "I just ain't gonna work in your daddy's church . . . that's *final*."

She looked up at him. "However you want it, lover-man." This time she did not move her leg when he reached for her knee. She lifted the movie magazine and began to read about a new actress named Joan Crawford, who, the article insisted, was destined for quick stardom.

Buck put his hand back on the wheel and began to sing again.

> "What a beautiful thought I am thinkin'
> Concernin' that great speckled bird. . . ."

The black sedan drew to a stop in front of the cabin in the motor court. Buck turned off the ignition.

"You sure this is the place?" Blanche asked petulantly, hoping it wasn't.

"Sure. Clyde don't make mistakes like that."

"It's awful quiet."

Buck grinned and winked broadly. "But not for long, darlin'." He punched at the horn in a military rat-tat-tat. Then again. The harsh blare cut through the still country air.

The door to the cabin was flung open and Clyde was framed in the opening. A wild cry of joy broke out of him and he ran for the car. Buck heaved himself from behind the wheel to meet his brother. Arms opened wide, they closed forcefully around each other, and each pounded at the other's back with what seemed like crippling force to Blanche. She grimaced.

"Buck!" Clyde crowed.

"Clyde! You son of a bitch!"

Blanche tried to close her ears to that kind of language. She intended to break Buck of that nasty habit as soon as she could. She watched without enthusiasm as the two brothers began to spar with each other, faking punches, blocking shadow blows, striking out in exaggerated slow motion, jabbing at each other's shoulders. Men, she thought, were so physical about so many things.

The sparring ceased, both men sucking air, laughing in short, almost reflexive bursts. "How's Ma?" Clyde got out.

"Just fine, just fine."

"How's sister?"

"Just fine, just fine. Send their best to you."

They stood a stride apart, studying each other. Clyde patted Buck's paunch. "Hey, you're fillin' out there. Must be that prison food."

Buck guffawed happily. "Hell, no, it ain't! It's married life, brother. You know what they say, it's the face powder that gets a man interested, but it's the bakin' powder that keeps him at home." A noisy explosion of sound erupted out of Buck, pleased with his own joke, and Clyde joined in.

"Hey, Buck, you are somethin', the best ol' joke-teller I ever did know."

Buck swung a low roundhouse at his brother's middle. "Hey! You just gotta meet my wife. Hey, honey, c'mon out here now and meet my baby brother."

Blanche climbed slowly out of the car, shielding her eyes from the sun with the movie magazine. She assessed Clyde obliquely and her mouth twitched in what might have been a smile.

"Howdydo?" she simpered.

Clyde reached out for her hand, shook it athletically. "Howdy-do. Sure is nice to know you."

Blanche rescued her hand just as Bonnie appeared in the doorway of the cabin. A single glance, then she stepped outside, the screen door slamming behind her. All heads swung in her direction and for an extended interval there was no movement, no sound.

It was Buck who interrupted the tableau. He bounded toward Bonnie, beaming and jolly, arms outstretched, voicing his pleasure.

"Well, now! You must be Bonnie!" His arms encircled her

53

in a gentle bearhug, then stepped back. "Now I hear you been takin' good care of the baby in the family. Well, sis, I'm real glad to meet you." He hugged her again and Bonnie submitted. "Saay," he said, releasing her. "I'd like for you to meet my wife, Blanche."

Bonnie stared stiffly at the other woman. "Hello."

Blanche was equally formal, equally stiff. "Hello," she replied.

There was a silent moment, awkward and unfilled, and a sense of hostility rose up around them all. It was C. W. who shattered the frozen scene. Wearing only his underwear, he cut a ludicrous figure, hair unkempt, eyes swollen with sleep, oblivious of the startling image he presented.

"How do, everybody," C. W. began.

Blanche took one look, averted her eyes, and backed off.

"Everybody," Clyde said. "This here is C. W. Moss. C. W., I want you to meet my brother Buck and his wife, Blanche."

"How do, y'all."

He shook hands with Buck and turned to Blanche, approaching her with simple-minded friendliness, unaware of the impact his appearance had had upon her. He took her hand.

"Well, how do, Mrs. Barrow," he said happily. "Or can I call you Blanche? I sure am pleased to meet you." Blanche rolled her eyes, seeking some avenue of escape from this wild-looking creature. "Did you have a hard time findin' us here in this neck of the woods? Well, you sure picked a good day for it. Say, is that the new *Screenland* you got there? Anything about Myrna Loy in it, any pictures or stories? She's my number-one favorite movin'-picture star."

Blanche shook her head in short, quick jerks, edging over to where Buck stood, trying to quell the panic that went seeping into her limbs. This young man in his BVDs, so strange, weird-looking and wild-sounding. He troubled her. Frightened her. She clutched anxiously at her husband's arm and held on tightly.

C. W. noticed none of it, grinning openly, his little eyes glowing in friendship. But Bonnie missed nothing and decided that there was a lot about Blanche Barrow she didn't like.

"Hey!" Buck cried. "How about us takin' some photographs? Lemme get the Kodak."

"That's a great idea, Buck!" Clyde said.

Buck hustled over to his car to return in a moment carrying a folding Brownie camera. He busied himself opening it and extending the bellows.

"We're gonna get us some fine snaps," he boasted.

Clyde fired a cigar and puffed contentedly. "Hey, C. W., go put on your pants. We're goin' to take some pictures."

C. W. scurried into the cabin.

"Y'all hear about the guy who thought Western Union was a cowboy's underwear?" Buck said, laughing at his own joke.

Clyde guffawed and faked a roundhouse at his brother's jaw. "Man, Buck, you are too much. Too much."

Buck grabbed Clyde by the arm and pulled him over to where Blanche stood. He guided Clyde's arm around her, pushing them close together.

"Now," he said. "Lemme get one of my bride and my brother."

Blanche giggled cutely, too cutely, Bonnie thought. "Buck! Don't you dare take my picture *now*. I'm just a mess from drivin' all day."

He reassured her. "Oh, honey, you look real fine."

"You really think so?"

"Sure. Doesn't she look fine, Clyde?"

"That's a fact, Blanche."

Buck snapped the picture.

"Did you actually take my picture?" Blanche said, feigning

girlish outrage that somehow failed to enhance her appearance. "Oh, Buck, I declare . . ."

Buck laughed and went over to Bonnie, guided her into position next to Clyde and Blanche. He stepped back and looked into the viewfinder.

"Let's have some big smiles, now."

Neither Bonnie nor Blanche softened her expression; Clyde alone smiled for the camera.

"Hey, Buck," Clyde said, pulling out his revolver and doing a Cagney pose. "Get one of this."

"Hold that," Buck said, snapping. "Clyde, now you do one of me and my missus."

Clyde aimed the camera while Buck put his arm around Blanche. "That does it," he said. "Now let me take one of Bonnie."

She grinned at him and took the cigar out of his mouth and thrust it between her own teeth at a rakish angle. "Okay, how's this?"

Clyde laughed.

Buck laughed.

Blanche watched coldly.

C. W. appeared in his jeans and jacket. "That's terrific, Bonnie," he said.

Clyde handed the camera to C. W. "Here, C. W., you take some pictures of the girls."

"That's right," Buck said. "It's time me and my baby brother had us a little talk."

"Don't be long, now, Buck." Blanche called after them. "You know how I hate to be alone without you, honey-love."

The two men went into the cabin and Buck closed the door behind them. Here it was dim and conspiratorial, the only light seeping from around the edges of the drawn shades. The two men stole looks at each other, swung half-punches, and toed the floor.

"Hey, Clyde . . ."

"Yeah . . ."

"Clyde." Buck kept his eyes averted. "It was you or him, wasn't it?"

"Huh?"

"That guy you killed. I mean, you had to do it, didn't ya? You *had* to." There was no disguising the anxiety in Buck's tone. He was telling Clyde clearly what he wanted to hear, what he wanted the truth to be.

Clyde ducked his head. He wanted to please his older brother, to protect him. He made a deprecatory gesture. "You know me, Buck. He put me in a spot, so I had to. The guy didn't have a Chinaman's chance."

"But you had to," Buck insisted.

"Yeah," Clyde agreed. "I had to."

Buck punched Clyde's shoulder lightly, pleased with the explanation. Then, confidentially: "There ain't no need to say nothin' to Blanche about it."

"Whatever you say, big brother. Hey, that time you broke out of jail, *she* talk you into goin' back?"

Buck couldn't conceal his embarrassment. He had hoped Clyde hadn't heard about that. "Yeah, you hear about that?"

Clyde shrugged it away. "I won't say nothin' to Bonnie about it."

"I appreciate it."

"Yeah . . . say, what d'ya think of Bonnie?"

"She's a real peach."

"Yeah . . . so's Blanche."

"Yeah. She's a preacher's daughter but she's okay and I love her a lot."

"Sure. You married her, didn't you?"

"That's right."

There was an extended pause and they gazed at each other, then turned away, each trapped by his own emotions, his own mélange of thoughts that refused to be isolated and spoken. For each of them there were words best buried and forgotten, best not voiced, and each wore his inhibitions like a suit of armor. The silence continued, thick, ponderous, a strain, too much to bear. It was Buck, the natural enemy of silence, who destroyed it, clapping his hands together and letting out an Indian war whoop.

"Whooeee!" he yelled.

"Whooeee!" Clyde echoed.

"Whooeee!"

Again the silence and again it was Buck who ended it.

"Boy," he said, supporting the words with all his energy. "Boy, are we gonna have us a time!"

"We surely are!"

"Yessir. A good ol' time."

"Yeah."

Buck hesitated. "What are we gonna do?"

"Well, how's this . . . I thought we'd all go up to Missouri. They ain't lookin' for me there. We'll hole up someplace and have us a regular vacation. All right?"

Buck looked up. "No trouble, now?"

"No trouble," Clyde said soberly. "I ain't lookin' to go back to prison."

"Hey," Buck said, his high spirits returning. "What's this I hear about you cuttin' up your toes, boy?"

"That ain't but half of it. I did it so I could get off work detail . . . breakin' those damned rocks with a hammer day and night. Sure enough, next week I got paroled. I walked out of that godforsaken jail on crutches."

"Shoot . . ."

Clyde went to the door and opened it. "Ain't life grand?" he laughed over his shoulder, before ducking out into the sunlight.

8

It was a good day, bright and sunny, and Clyde and Buck agreed that life was fine and that they didn't intend to be separated again. At least, not for a while. About fifty feet back trailed the second car with Bonnie, Blanche, and C. W.

They had set out for Joplin, Missouri, early that morning in Buck's car, along the main highway. Though traffic was light at this hour, Clyde drove carefully.

"No sense having some policeman hang a ticket on us for speedin', big brother," he had explained.

Buck had guffawed at that and slapped his knee. "One thing us Barrows don't want is trouble with the law," he agreed.

That had been earlier, when they started out. Now, cruising along a pleasant stretch of road through gentle hills, Buck was regaling his brother with a succession of jokes. Clyde made a fine audience—always had, in fact. He listened in silent anticipation and responded enthusiastically on cue.

"And the doc . . ." Buck said, developing the new story,

"he takes him aside, says, 'Son, your old mama's just gettin' weak and sickly layin' there. I want you to persuade her to take a little brandy, y'know, to pick her spirits up.' 'Why, doc,' he says, 'you know my mama is a teetotaler. She wouldn't touch a drop.' 'Well, I tell you what,' the doc says, 'why don't you bring her a fresh quart of milk every day from your farm, 'cept you fix it up so half of it's brandy and don't let on!' So he does that, doctors it up with brandy, and his mama drinks some of it. And the next day he brings it again and she drinks some more . . . and she keeps it up every day. Finally, one week later, he brings her the milk and don't you know she just swallows it all down, and looks at her boy and says, 'Son, whatever you do, *don't sell that cow!*' "

For a brief second there was silence inside the car, Buck watching Clyde in anticipation. Then the younger man exploded into loud laughter. His hands released the steering wheel and the car swerved wildly over to the wrong side of the road. Clyde managed to straighten it out, still laughing, tears forming rivulets down his smooth cheeks.

"Don't sell that cow!" he cackled. "Oh, Buck, you are somethin', man. Just somethin'."

Buck clapped his brother on the back. "Now listen to this one, Clyde. Seems there was this travelin' man . . ."

The atmosphere in the second car was starkly different, the silence oppressively thick and larded with animosity. Bonnie was driving, hunched forward, hands tight on the wheel, mouth set stubbornly, a cigarette angling aggressively from between her red lips. She glared at the road ahead as if it was an enemy, something to attack and conquer.

Blanche sat in the front seat, also, but against the door, having removed herself as far as possible from Bonnie. Her eyes watered from the cigarette smoke and her nose twitched disdainfully and she sent silent signals across the distance that separated them ordering Bonnie to extinguish the offending cigarette. It did no good. Finally, Blanche conceded defeat and rolled down the window, turning in that direction, breathing deeply, anxious to cleanse her lungs with some good, clean country air.

In the back seat, C. W. was curled up, feet higher than his head, staring sightlessly at some close point in space, oblivious of the two women, unaware of the tensions that separated them. C. W. was happy, as usual. A random thought wiggled around in the depths of his brain, rose to a more transparent level, and finally surfaced. The small mouth twitched joyfully.

"I ain't never been to Joplin, Missouri, before," he said.

"Oh, shut up, C. W.," Bonnie snapped.

C. W.'s face lengthened and he fell quiet. She had no call to talk to him that way. After all, he hadn't hardly said anything at all. Soon the resentment washed out of his face and he withdrew into that deep solitariness where he existed most of the time.

There was still a considerable portion of the afternoon remaining when they arrived in Joplin and Clyde had no trouble in finding the address he wanted. He drew the car over to one side and parked and watched as behind him Bonnie did likewise.

"All right, Buck," he said. "You know what to do."

"Sure do."

"I arranged everything by telephone, so just say it the way I told you."

From where they sat, looking past the tree-shaded house fronting the street, they could see down the driveway, which ended in a double garage; above it was an apartment. A dapper man in a white shirt, a bow tie, and a new straw hat stood in the entrance to the driveway playing with a set of keys.

"That figures to be the man," Clyde said. "The rental agent."

Buck nodded, got out of the car, and walked across the street.

"Howdo," he said to the man in the driveway. "You don't happen to be from the Jackson Realty Company?"

"Indeed I am. And you must be Mr. Hayes?"

"That's for damned sure," Buck said, offering his hand.

"Well, I'm pleased to meet you, Mr. Hayes." He extended one hand and dangled the keys. "Everything is ready for you, just as we discussed it." He cleared his throat and arranged a diffident smile on his thin mouth. "I believe that we agreed on the phone to one month's rent in advance."

"Right." Buck reached for his wallet and counted off some money. "Here y' are, Mr. Weeks."

The rental agent took a step toward the garage apartment. "I'll show you the premises."

"No need to," Buck said hurriedly, taking the keys from the other man. "Mighty good of you to discombobulate yourself this way . . ."

"Not at all. I hope you enjoy the apartment. Now you just call me if you need anything. Any help I can offer . . ."

"Matter of fact, there is somethin'. Anyplace around that'll deliver some groceries?"

"Sure. Smitty's on Marian Street. Just call 4337."

Clyde watched all this and only when Mr. Weeks had got into his own car and driven off did he get out. He glanced up and down the street, signaled to Bonnie, and began to unload their luggage.

Buck led the way into the apartment, carrying Blanche in his arms, as befitted a recent bride. The others came right behind, burdened down with suitcases.

"This is all right," Clyde said.

"Sure is," echoed C. W.

"C'mon," Bonnie put in irritably. "Let's get things straightened away." She headed for one of the bedrooms, Clyde following.

Blanche was more interested in the kitchen. She made a slow tour of the room, hand in hand with her husband.

"Oh, look, Buck," she cooed girlishly. "It's so clean.

And look at this here Frigidaire, not an icebox." She yanked open the door and her expression altered radically when she spotted a curl of ancient and wilted celery resting on the top shelf. She slammed the door shut. Bonnie, she told herself, could clean the Frigidaire later on. Her eyes traveled around the kitchen. "Oh, Buck, ain't this a bee-utee-full range?"

Buck had detached himself from his wife and was speaking into the telephone. "Operator ... I want Smitty's grocery store on Marian Street. The number? Oh, yeah, 4337 ..."

"Look at this counter, honey-love. It's got real linoleum on it. Ain't that clever, though?"

Buck spoke into the phone. "Is this Smitty's? Well, I want to give you an order, a big one. Can you deliver right away? All right, then. How about some pork chops? Eight pounds ought to do ... and four pounds of red beans ... and a can of Chase and Sanborn coffee ..." He laughed. "That's it, Eddie Cantor's coffee ... and some eggs, a couple of dozen ... some milk and eight bottles of Dr. Pepper and some Rice Krispies and ..."

Finished unpacking, they all gathered in the living room. Buck made himself comfortable in the big soft chair, his shoes off, and was soon engrossed in a newspaper. Blanche wandered around the room, touching this, eyeing that, spying dust in corners, fingering curtains and fluffing pillows. Across the room, Clyde was busy checking the action of his guns, reloading them carefully after wiping each bullet clean. C. W. was lost in the glamorous pages of a movie magazine. Bonnie sat staring into space wishing something would happen, offended by this tranquil setting.

"This sure is nice," Blanche murmured.

No one answered.

She came up behind her husband and looked down at his thinning locks. "Ain't it nice, lover?"

He grunted absently.

"My," Blanche said, pitching her voice girlishly high.

"You sure do need a haircut, Daddy. You look like a hill-billy boy." She ran her fingers through his hair.

Buck shook his head as if in protest, but he laughed with pleasure. "Now you stop messin' with my hair, now. Lemme read my paper in peace, Blanche."

"Just like an old man," she said. "Got his nose stuck in the paper, doesn't pay any attention to his poor little wife."

"Shucks, Blanche . . . c'mon now."

It was too much for Bonnie. She heaved herself erect, tension stiffening her body. Her eyes caught Clyde's and the quick movement of her head along with the tight look of disgust on her pretty face made him know that she wanted to talk to him alone. He trailed her into their bedroom, closing the door behind him.

Bonnie turned swiftly, reaching for his hair, rumpling it with mock ferocity. "Oh, Daddy," she cooed in an unmerciful imitation of Blanche. "You shore do need a haircut. You look just like a little ol' hillbilly boy, I do declare. Oh, mercy me, oh, my stars . . ."

Clyde glanced nervously at the door. "Hush up, Bonnie, willya? They're right in the next room."

Bonnie swung away from him. "Shoot, there's always somebody in this room, the next room, every other kind of room. We ain't never alone."

Clyde tried not to show the annoyance he suddenly felt. "That ain't no nice way to talk about my brother."

"I ain't talkin' about your brother," Bonnie said, falling into her imitation of Blanche. "If it was just your brother, I wouldn't say a single word. It's that Blanche . . ."

"Well, now, she's Buck's wife and . . ."

The coarse sound of the doorbell cut him short. He stiffened and his hand went to the gun in his belt. An oath broke out of Clyde and he flung the door open. Buck, Blanche, and C. W. were standing looking nervously to him for guidance. "Who the hell is that?" Clyde said.

"Take it easy," Bonnie said, moving past him. "It must be

the groceries. Y'all sit around and have yourselves a real good ol' time," she drawled, "and just leave everythin' to little ol' Bonnie." She went down the stairs to the front door. "Who is it?" she said.

"Groceries, ma'am," a voice answered.

She opened the door. A slender youth stood there, a big bag of groceries in each arm. She gave him her best smile. "Well, we sure are glad to see you. I was about to starve to death. How much do I owe you?"

"Six dollars and forty-three cents, ma'am."

She counted off the money, gave it to him, and reached for the brown bags.

"Them bags is heavy, ma'am," he said. "Let me carry them up the stairs for you."

"No, thanks," she said curtly. "I'll take them."

He shrugged and handed them over and watched her struggle up the stairs with the heavy burden. A puzzled look came over his boyish face. People were funny, the things they did sometimes, and didn't do . . . It made a fella think . . .

It was two hours later. They had eaten, the food helping to relax the tensions, to replenish their drained energies. They sprawled around the living room, all except Blanche, who was happily fussing in the kitchen, preparing for the evening meal.

Bonnie, who had been industriously writing in a note-book, one of those speckled black-covered books that schoolboys use, looked up.

"Anybody interested in hearin' a poem?" she asked shyly.

"Is that what you been doin'?" Clyde said. "Writin' a poem?"

"I never know'd you could write poetry, Bonnie," C. W. said, straightening up in admiration.

Bonnie cleared her throat. "It's called 'The Ballad of Suicide Sal.'" She paused, made certain she had their attention, and began to read.

"We each of us have a good alibi
For being down here in the joint;
But few of them really are justified
If you get right down to the point.
You've heard of a woman's glory
Being spent on a downright cur."

"Boy," Buck said. "You write that all by yourself?"
Her face tightened. "You want to hear this or not?"
"Well, sure," Buck said.
She glanced up at Clyde, who grinned proudly. She
turned back to the notebook and began to read softly.

"Still you can't always judge the story
As true, being told by her.
As long as I've stayed on this island
And heard confidence tales from each gal,
Only one seemed interesting and truthful—
The story of Suicide Sal.
Now Sal was a gal of rare beauty,
Though her features were coarse and tough—"

Buck couldn't restrain himself. "Yeah," he broke in. "I
knew her. She was cockeyed and had a harelip and no
teeth!"
One penetrating look from Bonnie and his mouth clamped
shut. She took a deep breath and went on.

"Now Sal was a gal of rare beauty,
Though her features were coarse and tough;
She never once faltered from duty
To play on the up and up."

Slowly, very slowly, and very quietly, Clyde lifted
himself out of his chair. Listening, enjoying every word,
finding silent pleasure in Bonnie's talent, in the sweet sound

of her voice, he moved behind her, placing each foot carefully, anxious to do nothing to shatter the mood.

Outside the apartment there was also movement, equally quiet, equally anxious to disturb nothing. At least, not yet. Two police cars pulled up to the curb just out of sight of the garage apartment. A lieutenant led his men out of the cars, giving a brief command to the driver of the first car, who eased his vehicle forward so that it blocked the entrance to the driveway.

The lieutenant signaled his men to take up positions, to find suitable cover before moving in. They obeyed, men ready for anything, guns drawn, faces grim and determined. The lieutenant checked his people and was dissatisfied. He motioned for a couple of men to move forward, closer to the garage itself, and one other to take up a position with an unobstructed line of sight to the apartment entrance.

In the apartment, Bonnie was still reading "The Ballad of Suicide Sal." Concentrating on the words, Clyde stepped away, over to the window. He looked out. A sudden movement caught his eye, a flash of police blue, a gun hand extended, a gleaming badge. He blinked in disbelief. It couldn't be. They had been so cautious, careful not to attract any attention.

> "Sal told me this tale on the evening
> Before she was turned out free,
> And I'll do my best to relate it
> Just as she told it to me—"

Clyde swore.
"Look here, Clyde Barrow," Bonnie began.
"It's the law," he ripped out.
The words sliced through the air, to linger, a persistent echo, rising and falling in a penetrating wail that impelled them all to action. Guns leaped into hands and oaths broke out and there was the brittle shattering of windows.

"We can't let 'em take us!" Clyde cried, squeezing off the first shot.

At once all was chaos, a hysterical stoppage of time, all crashing sound as hammers fell against firing pins, pins driving fiercely into the caps of bullets. There were commands, hoarse cries, shouts of anger, of fear, of pain.

Blanche, in the kitchen, clapped her hands over her ears, a shrill scream streaming out of her gaping mouth, seeming to persist with no lessening of force, a shriek of despair, of total panic, a thin protest of terror, an unanswered cry for aid.

Clyde leveled on a blue chest in the driveway. He fired twice. The blue man catapulted backward. Dead. Another policeman ran across the driveway. C. W. gunned him down. Bonnie blazed away at a place in the shrubbery and saw a body plunge forward.

"We got to get out of here!" Clyde cried.

"They've got the driveway blocked off," Bonnie yelled.

"We got to try!"

"I'll go first!" Buck said.

He ran for the front door, the others close behind. Once outside, Buck ducked into the garage, firing as he went. The others were at his heels.

"Get in the car!" Buck yelled.

He went back outside, crouching, shooting at anything that moved. A policeman stepped into the open, took aim. Buck shot from the hip. The cop toppled over and lay still. Firing as he moved, Buck scuttled down the driveway to the police car that blocked their sole route of escape. Miraculously, no bullet even grazed him. He reached inside and released the handbrake, shoving hard at the car, watching it roll slowly down the incline and out of the way.

During all this, Blanche, still screaming, fled the apartment and went running away, untouched by the storm of bullets around her, desperate to escape the crescendo of sound and death, weaving blindly down the tree-lined street.

In the garage, in the car, Bonnie sat anxiously behind the wheel, Clyde beside her and C. W. in the back seat, both shooting wildly. "Now." Clyde cried. "Let's get out of here!"

Bonnie gunned the car and it shot ahead, the rear door on Buck's side open. At the street, she stepped down ferociously on the brake. The car screeched to a stop and Buck leaped head-first into the back and they were off again. Now the police left their hiding places, to fire after the car, and two of them went down in the answering volley.

Bonnie squinted at the street ahead. A wavering, weaving figure appeared, running loosely as if all its joints refused to mesh, as if its muscles and tendons had abdicated their strength. It was Blanche, still screaming.

"Let's get her!" Clyde ordered.

Buck glanced out the back window. "Ther're comin' after us, and fast."

"Keep shootin'," Clyde said grimly. He opened his door.

Bonnie maneuvered the car close to Blanche, then mashed down on the brake. Clyde reached and grabbed, pulled the hysterical woman inside. A second later they were speeding away. Behind them, a police car was closing fast and the ominous whistle of police bullets whirred dangerously close.

9

THEY WERE speeding through open countryside now, the two cars careering wildly from one side of the road to the other, bullets whizzing by. It was C. W., firing out the rear window, who ended the chase. He put a slug through the windshield of the pursuing vehicle, a slug that killed the driver instantly. The police cruiser veered sharply off the road and crashed head-on into a tree.

C. W. turned around. "They ain't followin' us now," he said coolly.

The words barely penetrated Clyde's brain. His foot continued heavy on the gas pedal and the speedometer hovered past 90. Behind him, pressing herself furiously against Buck, Blanche moaned and cried, mumbling incoherently.

Bonnie held herself very still, trying to close out the sound of the other woman. Finally, able to tolerate no more, she whirled around, face distorted, eyes blazing.

"Dammit!" she bit off. "You almost got us all killed! Makin' us come after you thataway."

Blanche began to sob louder. "What did I do wrong? I s'pose you'd be happier if I got shot."

"Yeah," Bonnie said thinly. "It'd save us all a lot of trouble."

"Buck," wailed Blanche. "Don't let that woman talk to me like that."

Buck grimaced. His nerves were still drawn tight; yet here he was caught in a delicate situation between his new wife and his brother's girlfriend.

"You shouldn't have done it, Blanche," he said, keeping his voice soft, trying to soothe her. "I mean, we're together, all of us, and we got to stay together, see?"

She gazed up into his face. "Please, Buck," she implored. "I didn't marry you to see you get all shot up. Please, Buck, let's go. Let's get out of here and leave. Make him stop the car and let us out."

Buck's eyes were somber and he turned to the front, staring at the back of Clyde's head. "Clyde," he said gravely. "Stop the car."

Without a word, Clyde obeyed, drawing over to the side of the road. Buck got out and motioned for Clyde to join him. Side by side, they moved across the shoulder onto the grassy slope that led into a stand of birch trees. Each of them felt the emotion of the other, emotion that bound them, and now threatened to rip them apart. Each of them understood instinctively that this moment was a crisis and each of them wanted to do nothing that would sunder familial ties.

Clyde stopped about six feet from the line of trees. He scuffed the earth, unable to look at Buck. His voice, when he spoke, was almost inaudible. Soft. Polite.

"Buck, you can't go and leave me. Not now."

"Oh, boy, Clyde . . . you sure screwed me good."

"You can't leave me, Buck."

Buck kicked at a clod of loose earth. He shook his head regretfully. "You told me time and again there wasn't goin' to be no trouble. An' now all this has happened and I am up the creek without a paddle."

Clyde walked in a tight little circle, head down.

71

Buck said, "I promised that sweet woman I'd change my ways."

Clyde stopped circling. "You can't leave."

Buck considered that. "Hey, Clyde," he summoned, voice very soft.

Clyde lifted his head. He never saw the roundhouse right Buck threw, the big fist catching him alongside the jaw, putting him flat on the grass. He lay without moving.

After appraising his fallen brother for a suitable interval, Buck helped him to his feet. He brushed dirt off his back, looped his arm across Clyde's shoulders, and sighed.

"Okay, Clyde. I reckon you're the boss."

They drove cautiously for the remainder of the day and into the next afternoon, hitting the dusty back roads, anxious to attract no attention, to fade from official sight. They tried to figure out how the police had found them, why the Joplin people had been interested in them. They found out when they came across an RFD mailbox with a newspaper sticking out of it. Clyde pulled alongside and Buck, in the back seat, appropriated the paper. He began to read.

"Hey, y'all," he said, voice rising jubilantly. "Listen to what it says here. 'Clyde Barrow, phantom desperado of the Southwest, fled before a growing army of police today after a gun battle on the streets of Joplin, Missouri, which saw the death of three policemen . . .'."

"Oh, Lord," Blanche moaned.

Clyde said nothing but a pained expression set in around his mouth. "Go on, Buck," he said quietly.

Buck continued to read. " 'Acting on a tip from a delivery boy, who said he suspected a bootlegging operation going on in a second-story apartment . . .' "

"Well, ain't that a crock?" C. W. said mildly.

"The whole thing," Bonnie muttered. "A mistake."

Buck went on, " '. . . Joplin police found themselves engaged in combat with the notorious Barrow gang. Chief

Percy Hammond expressed belief that among the gang was Barrow's brother, Buck, recently released from Huntsville Penitentiary' " Buck broke off. "Shoot," he growled.

"Go on," Bonnie said.

Buck did. "'A third man was unidentified. Chief Hammond also positively identified Bonnie Parker as the woman in the gang. Slain were Constables E. L. Kinsey, 35, Walter Edmonson, 27, and Deputy Carl Bender, 28. . . .'"

"Clyde," C. W. interrupted. "We ain't goin' to see a restroom for another thirty miles on this here road. Why don't you just stop here?"

Clyde nodded in relief. There was an increasing pressure on his bladder. He pulled the car into a wooded area on the far side of a quiet lake and stopped. A moment later he was out of the car, vanishing into the thick greenery.

Buck turned back to the newspaper. "Hey, now, here's somethin'," he said, laughing. Listen here: 'Lone Cop Arrests Two Officers in Hunt for Barrow. Police officer Howard Anderson's heart turned faster than his motorcycle when he forced to the side of the road a roaring black V-8 sedan in which were three men and a blonde-headed woman yesterday afternoon.'" They all laughed at that and Buck continued to read. "'When he saw several machine guns in the car he was certain he'd caught Clyde Barrow, Bonnie Parker, and maybe Buck Barrow and the third unidentified member of the gang. It took a lot of telephoning and explaining to convince the motorcycle cop that his captives were two highway patrolmen and a blonde-haired stenographer from the Highway Patrol.'" He broke into loud laughter, the four of them enjoying the thought of the discomfort caused the police when they saw this story in the papers. It was the first light moment they had experienced since the battle in Joplin and perhaps they laughed too loud, too long, anxious to hold on to the pleasure they felt, the relief.

None of them thought to look around, to stay alert to possible danger. And so none of them noticed when a police car pulled to a quiet stop on the road. Nor did any of them see the tall Texas Ranger get out, his big hand drawing his .45, as he moved stealthily toward their car until he was close enough to hear Buck's voice continuing to read.

" 'Anderson was held up as an example for every other peace officer today. "That was a mighty brave thing," explained Highway Patrol Chief L. C. Winston.' "

Clyde finished relieving himself and started back toward the car. He moved with no particular speed, enjoying this pastoral interlude, listening idly to the low drone of his brother's voice, trying to think ahead, plan their next step. They would have to find someplace to lay over, some safe, out-of-the-way place. He stepped out of the woods and went cold. Ahead of him, no more than twenty feet, gun in hand, was the impressive silhouette of a Texas Ranger. Clyde drew his pistol and brought it to bear, eyes narrow. A part of him seemed to stand off and watch, as if he were a player in a Western movie. Here they were, the good guy and the bad guy smack in the middle of the main street of town, about to fast draw each other.

"Sheriff!" he rasped.

The Ranger spun, knees bent, .45 searching for the target. Fingers tightened on triggers and two shots crashed out, almost simultaneously. The Ranger grunted and the pistol went flying out of his hands. He straightened and rubbed his numb right hand, eyeing Clyde as he moved forward.

The others came rushing from the car, guns ready, but it was all over.

"Boy," C. W. gushed. "What a shot, Clyde!"

"Christ almighty," Buck crowed. "I never seen shootin' like that, boy!"

C. W. and Buck took hold of the tall Ranger and pulled his arms behind his back, using his own handcuffs to immobilize him. They backed him violently over the rear of the sedan, roughing him up. Buck picked up the .45 and held it aloft, a trophy of victory.

"What are we goin' to do with him now that we got him?" he said.

The Ranger gave no sign that he was affected by any of this or that their words penetrated in any way. His strong, seamed face remained impassive and his far-sighted eyes stared straight ahead. His handlebar mustache added to the sense of self-sufficiency and power if the man.

"Well," Buck said in mock courtesy, his politeness exaggerated. "Ain't this somethin' now. Us entertainin' a gen-u-ine Texas Ranger. Ain't you a long piece from home?"

Clyde leaned forward, grinning tightly, holding the muzzle of his pistol under the Ranger's chin. "Say there, peacemaker. I am Clyde Barrow and this here little lady is Bonnie Parker and you are with the Barrow gang. I reckon you heard of us."

The Ranger gave no sign that he had heard, the big face implacable, the full mouth firmly closed, registering no emotion.

Buck gave a low bow. "We're mighty honored to have a honest-to-God Texas Ranger with us. Now ain't you honored to be with the Barrow gang?"

Again no reply.

Buck went on. "How big are you, Ranger? About nine feet tall, I'd say."

The Ranger stared into space.

"He don't say nothin', this here Texas Ranger," C. W. put in.

Clyde measured the man. "Can't you speak at all, lawman?"

"Listen," Buck said, "we don't want you to get the wrong impression of us. We 'bout the most polite folks in the world. And just as friendly as pie, ain't we, Clyde?"

"Sure we are. Say, Buck, let's us show the Ranger here how friendly we are. Let's all take our picture with him, just to be neighborly."

"That's a terrific idea."

"We can take pictures and send the pictures to the news-papers," Bonnie added. "Wouldn't you like that, Sheriff?" She sidled closer, looking the tall man over.

Buck fetched his camera and posed Clyde and Bonnie, Blanche and C. W. on either side of the Ranger, pressing close to the man, showing their guns, grinning and making comic faces, while he snapped away. C. W. snatched the Ranger's badge from his chest, pinned it to his own shirt.

"Lookee here. I'm a Texas Ranger."

"Well, now," Clyde said. "I'm mighty proud to have a Texas Ranger in the family. Hey, man," he said to the law-man, "why don't you swear him in as an official Ranger?" There was no response. "C'mon, Ain't you never goin' to say *anything?*"

"Bet I can make him talk," Bonnie injected, pushing closer to the Ranger.

"Go ahead, Bonnie," C. W. urged. "Make him talk."

Clyde thought he saw a flicker of something in the big man's face. Distaste? Fear? He laughed thinly.

"Make him talk, Bonnie."

Bonnie stepped up to the Ranger, ran her hands lightly over the broad chest, across his stomach, back up again, stroking lightly at his throat.

"Take your hands off me!" the Ranger said with low intensity.

"There!" Buck laughed. "He can talk. I knew it."

"Me, too," C. W. guffawed. "I knew it too."

"What are we goin' to do with him?" Clyde said, sud-denly losing interest in this game.

But Bonnie wasn't finished. There was a strange kind of pleasure to be extracted from this, an alien excitement, and she wasn't yet prepared to let it go. She stretched until her face was close to the Ranger's and in a swift motion her mouth came down, smashing against his full lips, forcing herself upon him, into him, her tongue alive against his teeth, her breasts flat and hot to his chest, her belly pressing against

76

his loins. At last she pulled back, breathless and aware of the tingling passion spreading under her skin.

Buck laughed loudly.

And C. W.

And Clyde. But there was no humor in the sound he made.

For a long, thick second, everything was still; then the Ranger reached back into some deep well of privacy and spat his loathing into Bonnie's face.

She gasped and fell back.

Clyde erupted with frightening intensity, grabbing the Ranger by the shirt front, whirling him around, reaching for his gun, intending to pistol-whip the helpless man. Buck snatched the gun away. That failed to stop Clyde, who had gone wild, was swinging both fists at the Ranger, cursing him, shouting imprecations at the top of his voice. Only his own raging anger kept him from doing real injury to the handcuffed lawman.

The Ranger fell backward to the ground and rolled as Clyde launched a kick at his exposed side. He missed and fell himself, scrambling after the other man. Together they went sliding and slipping down to the edge of the lake, neither able to gain purchase in the thick ooze in the shallows.

Buck came after them, and C. W., clutching at Clyde, trying to pull him away. He broke loose and charged the helpless Ranger again, pulling him erect, heaving him backward, crashing into a rowboat pulled halfway up on shore, tumbling into it. Clyde was on him, pummeling away, heaving him all the way into the boat.

Buck and C. W. saw his intentions and moved to help, working the boat free, shoving it into the lake, where it floated silently upon the still waters, the Ranger's big rugged face peering back at them over the side.

"Remember us!" Clyde shouted. "The Barrow gang. We'll send those pictures of you to the newspapers so everybody'll know what good friends we are. Oh, yes, you remember us!"

They took hold of Clyde, C. W. and Buck, and moved him back toward the car. Before getting in, Clyde turned to Bonnie and smiled wanly. "That Ranger," he murmured. "He wasn't any fun at all."

"No," she agreed very softly. "No fun at all."

They drove away without looking back and so failed to see the Ranger sitting erect in the boat, the bony face set, the pale eyes glittering with hatred and the desire for revenge.

10

THEY KEPT running, spending extended hours in the cars, sleeping in fourth-rate motor courts in out-of-the-way places where they were unlikely to be spotted. Soon it became evident to them all that they could not go on this way for one single, pressing reason—they were running out of money. To Clyde, that meant only one thing and he told them so.

"We're going to stick up a bank," he announced.

"Oh, no!" Blanche gasped.

"Well, now," C. W. said mildly, his little mouth curled happily. "That is a good thing."

"What bank you thinkin' about, brother?" Buck asked.

And Bonnie looked at Clyde with pride and pleasure in her blue eyes.

"It's a place I spotted," Clyde told them, "some distance back, when we was doubling back and forth. It looked good to me and I been thinkin' on it and now I decided. We do it tomorrow."

They parked behind a windbreak dividing two farms that night, taking no chances on being recognized. And the next afternoon, they prepared for the job ahead. Buck and Blanche were ready before the others and climbed into the back seat to wait, even while C. W. continued to work on the engine, checking every part, anxious that if anything went wrong he would not be to blame.

Bonnie, neatly dressed as if on her way to an afternoon tea, fussed with her hair, looking into a hand mirror propped up on the fender. Clyde stood behind her adjusting the knot in his tie.

"Oh, what I wouldn't give for naturally curly hair," Bonnie mumbled.

Clyde looked at himself in the mirror. "Hey, Bonnie, you like this shirt or the other one better?" He held up a striped shirt on a hanger.

Bonnie straightened up and appraised each shirt. "That one." She pointed to the one on the hanger.

"Yeah, you're right."

He unbuttoned his shirt, tossed it aside, donned the other one, tied his tie. He checked himself in the mirror again and approved of what he saw.

C. W. came around to where they stood, wiping his greasy hands on his jeans. "Engine's all tuned and ready to go. Say, don't you two look swell, like a couple of dudes."

Bonnie glared at him disapprovingly. "C. W., are you goin' to go like that?"

"Sure. What's wrong?"

She shook her head sadly. "Boy, you just have to learn to dress right, with a sense of style. Look at Clyde."

"Yeah, ain't he something?"

Clyde slipped on his jacket.

From inside the car, Buck yelled, "Hey, y'all! Shake a leg. That bank's goin' to be closed up tighter'n a miser's purse by the time we get there."

"We're comin'," Clyde said.

"Boy," Buck said, "I never seen people get so gussied up to rob a bank."

Clyde climbed into the front seat, Bonnie beside him. C. W. took his place behind the wheel.

"When that bank president goes to work," Clyde told Buck, "he dresses to suit his position. And when I go in to take his money, I dress to suit mine."

"Well, let's go!" Bonnie said. A moment later they were on their way.

C. W. stayed with the car, behind the wheel, engine purring and ready to move out. Blanche was in the back seat, drawn tight and pale, eyes darting nervously from the bank entrance to the street, seeing every moving figure as a policeman, anticipating disaster.

Inside the bank things went smoothly. Buck led the way, heading directly for the chief teller's cage, Bonnie moving to the window alongside. Clyde brought up the rear, perceiving the entire scene, drawing his two pistols and announcing in a loud, pleasant voice, "This is the Barrow gang, folks, so everybody just take it easy and nobody will get hurt."

The customers, at the cashiers' windows, at the loan desk, preparing deposits, all straightened up in place, faces slack with fear, hands rising uncertainly.

"That's it, folks," Clyde said. "Get your hands up. Makes it all easier and safer."

Bonnie heaved the sack she carried onto the counter and smiled at the teller in a winning fashion. "Fill 'er up, please."

The teller, a lady with a prim, disapproving mouth, hesitated. Bonnie gestured with her gun. "I said fill 'er up."

"Oh, yes. Yes, Miss. Right away."

Buck ducked behind the partition and pushed one teller aside, emptying the cash drawers, moving from one position to the next.

It was the prim-mouthed teller who, certain no one was watching her, stepped toward the alarm button, reached tentatively. At once something cold and ominous touched her bare wrist. She shuddered and turned to see Buck leering at her disapprovingly.

"Now, ma'am, if you was to touch that button we'd have an awful lot of company and we ain't prepared to entertain just now. I reckon you understand."

The thin head bobbed energetically and the thin mouth worked, but no sounds came out.

From his position near the front door, Clyde was able to see everything, the people in line, the executives at their desks, the bank guard, hands held at shoulder level and still wearing his pistol, a farmer with a handful of bills clutched in one thorny fist.

"That your money," Clyde said, "or the bank's?"

The farmer stared back unafraid. "It's my money, mister, hard earned too."

"Keep it then."

Clyde's eyes roamed beyond the farmer to where Bonnie was shoveling cash into her sack. Everything seemed to be going well, but he wished they would work faster.

"Speed it up," he called.

That was the chance the bank guard was waiting for. His right hand flashed to his gunbelt. Out of the corner of his eye, Clyde saw the movement. He whirled and fired in one motion. The hat atop the guard's head spun wildly and fell to the floor. The guard swallowed hard and his face went white.

"Next time," Clyde said matter-of-factly, "I'll aim a little lower."

"Not gonna be a next time," the guard muttered hoarsely.

"Let's finish it up," Clyde called.

"I'm about ready, Clyde," Buck called.

"Bonnie?"

She flashed a quick grin. "I guess I got all I can handle. Any time you're ready, Clyde."

"All right, then. Let's go."

They backed toward the entrance. Bonnie went first, Clyde and Buck covering her exit. A well-dressed middle-aged lady with a look of offended propriety on her chiseled face clutched an expensive beaded handbag to her ample bosom. As Buck passed her on his way out, he snatched the purse away.

The lady gasped.

"Thank you, ma'am," he said, and was gone.

Clyde followed close behind.

Seeing them, C. W. threw the doors of the car open and the gang went sprawling inside. C. W. hit the gas and they zoomed off down the street.

Buck tossed the handbag into Blanche's lap. "Happy birthday, honey," he cooed.

She smiled a pleased smile at the unexpected gift. "Why, lover, that was awful sweet of you to remember . . ."

Shots crashed out behind them and Blanche screamed and jammed her fingers into her ears as Bonnie, Clyde and Buck began firing out of the windows.

They reached the edge of town before the wail of a police siren reached them, closing fast. Clyde busied himself reloading his revolver.

"Kick it in the pants, C. W.," Buck said. "That's the law crowdin' behind us."

"We got to make that state line!" Clyde said grimly. "Those coppers ain't got the authority to cross into another state. C'mon, C. W., give 'er the gas."

C. W., bent over the wheel, fighting to keep the car under control on the bumpy and potted road, kept his eyes fastened to the front. "Can't get more'n this out of a Plymouth! Tol' you we shoud've got us somethin' bigger and faster."

And back at the bank, the guard, collar open, holding his pistol in his right hand, seemed to be enjoying himself. A crowd had collected around him.

"Then he saw me goin' for my gun" the guard repeated for the fourth time. "Clyde Barrow hisself, I mean. And suddenly I was starin' into the face of death!"

"But you never faltered, Mr. Hawkins," cooed a lady teller.

He nodded solemnly. "I seen my duty and I done it."

A photographer raised his camera. "Just look this way, Mr. Hawkins."

The guard nodded amiably, buttoning his collar and smiling into the lens.

A rabbit went skittering across the road and the Plymouth skidded as C. W. hit the brake, speeded up again at once.

"You tryin' to kill us, C. W.?" Buck said, turning a reassuring expression in his wife's direction. She had her eyes squeezed tight and her fingers still deep in her ears.

"Watch where you're drivin'," Clyde said.

"It was a rabbit. I couldn't run down a rabbit."

A shot whizzed past. Another.

"Those police are closin' in," Bonnie said.

In the police cruiser, the two blue-clad men turned grim faces toward the car they were chasing. Each of them was aware of the importance of the gang they were chasing, of what it could mean to make such an important arrest. The man beside the driver hawked his throat clear and snapped a shot after the fleeing car.

"Step on it, Randolph," he said. "We gotta catch 'em 'fore they reach the state line."

And back at the bank, the bank president, a well-fed, portly man stood with his arm across the guard's shoulders pointing to a bullet hole in the wall. The photographer's flash exploded and the bank president removed his arm.

"All right, there's work to be done around here. Time's money, y'know. Time's money."

Buck leaned out the back window and took aim on the police car. He fired twice, pulled his head inside.

"Missed, dammit! Car jiggled my gun hand."

"Are we goin' to make the state line?" Bonnie said, a note of concern in her voice for the first time.

He didn't look at her. "C. W.'s doin' the best he can."

A shot sounded and the slug ricocheted off the rear fender. Blanche screamed.

"Oh, shut up!" Bonnie bit off. "Shut up!"

And back at the bank, the woman whose purse Buck had taken was talking to a reporter.

"Let me see, now," she mused. "There was my coin purse, of course, and a half-ounce bottle of toilet water, an excellent brand, and there were thirty Lucky Premium coupons. And there was . . ." Her hand went to her mouth and she blushed. "Oh, my *goodness!*"

"Here come those cops," Buck warned.

"And there's the state line up ahead," Clyde exulted.

The car seemed to bound ahead under C. W.'s urging and a half minute later they passed into the adjoining state.

Clyde exhaled audibly. "Okay, folks, you can all relax. We're in Oklahoma now. Slow down."

"What if the police keep after us?" C. W. asked.

Clyde glanced at him skeptically. "And break the law? Not a chance."

The police car sped across the state line without hesitation. "I think we're gonna get 'em," the driver said.

"Turn around," his colleague said. "Don't waste no more gas."

"Ain't we gonna catch 'em?"

"Hell, they're over the state line. That's out of our jurisdiction."

"Why don't we get 'em anyway?"

"I ain't gonna risk my life in Oklahoma. That's their problem."

They turned back.

The road was narrow and seemingly endless as it sliced through corn fields eye-high. No one had spoken for a long time. It was as if a deep and somber reaction to the tension and trepidation had at last set in and only time would bring them back to where they normally existed. It was C. W., unperturbed and happy, who broke the mood.

"How much money you reckon we got, Clyde?"

"Yeah, Clyde," Buck put in. "How much?"

Clyde took a long, thin cigar out of his pocket, bit off one end, and spat it out the window. Carefully, shielding the match with both hands, he puffed until the cigar was lit. He blew a great cloud of smoke and behind him Blanche coughed her displeasure.

"Let's see what we got," he said. "Pull over."

The car swerved to the side of the road, bounced across the ditch, and came to a stop on a stretch of open ground alongside the cornfield. They all got out and sat in the shade of the Plymouth and Clyde dumped all the money in a pile. He looked at it without enthusiasm.

"Hell," he said. "That ain't much, is it?"

Buck clucked sympathetically. "Times is hard."

"Crime doesn't ever pay," Blanche said righteously.

Bonnie glared at her but said nothing.

"Well," Clyde sighed. "Let's get to it."

He made himself comfortable on the running board and began to deal out bills as if dealing a poker hand. "This one's for Clyde Barrow," he said, laying down a bill. "And this one's for Buck Barrow . . . Bonnie Parker . . . and C. W. Now one more time . . . Clyde, Buck . . . Bonnie . . . C. W. . . . . Clyde . . . Buck . . . Bonnie . . . C. W. . . ."

Watching, her mouth turned down in a tight, disapproving purse, Blanche stood up and walked over to one side. With a quick jerk of her head, she brought Buck hurrying over.

"What is the matter, honey?" he inquired. "Is something the matter?"

"Look at that," she husked out angrily. "Look at what that brother of yours is doin'. Not givin' me a thing, not a solitary thing."

Buck shuffled his feet. "I tol' you I'd talk to Clyde and I will. First chance I get."

"Now," she insisted.

"Well—"

"Now is the time."

Buck stepped forward, Blanche at his shoulder. He placed an ingratiating smile on his face. "Uh . . . Clyde? Say, Clyde?"

"Yeah, Buck." Clyde continued to count.

"Y'see, Clyde . . . well . . . I been meanin' to talk to you about this."

"About what, Buck?"

"It's Blanche . . ."

Clyde looked up. "What about Blanche?"

"Well, Clyde, I been thinkin'. She should get her share."

Bonnie's face became mottled with rage. "*What!*"

Blanche realized that she would have to rise to her own defense and did so with unaccustomed spirit. "Well, why not? Say, I earned my share! Same as everybody. I coulda got killed by the laws same as everybody. Besides, I coulda got snakebite sleepin' in them woods all them nights."

Bonnie snorted her distaste. "Any snake bit you, honey-love, *he'd* get poisoned."

Blanche swung around. "I declare you're the meanest woman I ever knew."

"And you're the dumbest," Bonnie shot back.

"I may not be the smartest woman in the world, but I ain't no cheap tramp!"

"Come on, stop it," Clyde said.

C. W. smiled and said, "Let's all be friendly."

It was no use.

The rage in Bonnie had been collecting for too long, a rage and frustration that targeted on Blanche. She reached for her gun and leveled it at Blanche. "Okay, you bitch! How'd you like me to pull this trigger?"

"Hey," Buck yelled. "Put that gun down!"

"Aw, please, Bonnie," C. W. added plaintively.

It was Clyde who ended it, and triggered something else. He leaped to his feet, face livid, eyes squinting hotly. "I've had about all of this here temperament I am goin' to take, Bonnie. Now you just put that gun down and be quiet, hear!"

Bonnie's eyes skipped from face to face. No sympathy was evident anywhere. Clearly everyone had turned against her, transformed her into a stranger in an alien world, unloved, unwanted, and suddenly she had to get away, had to find some safe place among people she could depend on.

"Awright," she bit off. "I know when I'm not wanted." She fought for breath. "You can all go to hell."

She reached into the back seat of the car and pulled out a paper sack stuffed with her clothes. Furiously, she swung away, tripping, swearing, moving on.

"Where do you think you're goin' in the middle of nowhere?" Clyde called after her.

"I'm goin' home to my mama!"

They all laughed at that, even Clyde. And that solidified Bonnie's resolve, her frustration, and her anger. She broke into a run, darting into the corn field.

"You're makin' a fool out of yourself!" Clyde shouted.

There was no answer and seconds later she was gone among the tall stalks. Clyde sat back down on the running board.

C. W. looked at him. 'Ain't you goin' to go after her Clyde?" he said worriedly.

Clyde lit a cigar and puffed it contentedly. "She'll be back in ten minutes," he said confidently.

But she wasn't.

11

An hour passed and Bonnie did not appear. There was no laughter now and a crease of concern appeared between Clyde's eyes. Whatever had been troubling Bonnie, he had done nothing to ease her torment. He held himself responsible for the continuing conflict between her and Blanche. After all, he told himself, he was in charge of them all and made decisions for them all. He glanced at his watch for the tenth time in the last two minutes.

"Where the hell is she? She should've come back by now."

"Aw," Buck drawled. "That Bonnie, ain't nothin' can do her harm."

"Well, where is she?" Clyde stood up and pounded his fist into his hand. "Okay, let's take off. Everybody into the car. We're goin' to find Bonnie."

C. W. drove slowly down the narrow road between the cornfields as they scoured the tops of the tall stalks for some movement that might hint of Bonnie's presence.

"Anybody see anything?" Clyde said.

No one answered. They drove on. Suddenly, Buck, in

the back seat, leaned forward, squinting against the glare. "Lookee there! Into the sun. Ain't that somethin'?"

Clyde peered in that direction. "It's her!"

Not waiting for the car to stop, Clyde leaped out, dashing into the field, calling her name. At first sound of his voice, Bonnie broke into a run but he soon overtook her.

"No," she gasped. "Go away, Clyde Barrow. Leave me be. I'm through with you . . . all of you."

"Bonnie wait!"

"I . . . am . . . goin' . . . home . . . to . . . my . . . mama!"

She ordered her legs to move faster but the muscles refused to obey. A weakness flooded her limbs and the paper bag filled with clothes fell to the ground, breaking open. Her things were scattered over a wide area. Gasping for breath, she struggled ahead as Clyde came pounding up behind her. She avoided his initial lunge but her foot hooked into something and she went sprawling, out of breath, weak, helpless. Deep, racking sobs, spasms of despair, shook her entire body.

Then he was there, embracing her, covering her face with kisses, murmuring soothing sounds, stroking her hair, ignoring her protests, telling her how much he cared, how important he held her to be, his growing need for her, how scared and empty he was without her.

"Hey, Bonnie . . . hey, hey, hey, baby, don't cry, baby, hey, Bonnie . . . hey, that's better, now . . . hey, hey now, baby . . ."

She fought to speak but the words lodged in her throat.

"Don't ever do that again, Bonnie," he murmured. "You really scared me."

"I . . . I mean it, Clyde. I want . . . to see my . . . mama. Please. Please, Clyde. I want to see my mama. I want to see my mama. I want to see my mama."

He kissed her mouth to quiet her. "Yes, sweetheart, yes."

"I want to see my mama."

"Yes sweetheart."

Arrangements had to be made. Clyde was convinced the Texas Rangers were keeping a watch on the Parker family, waiting for the Barrow gang to show up. Phone calls were made and strategy mapped and it was eventually agreed to meet in the open, where it would be impossible to be ambushed, so if necessary an escape could be made.

The entire Parker family showed in a field to the north of West Dallas, a field not far from the good road, as if coming together for a picnic, with food and drink and all the children. The day was not good for a picnic, gray and overcast, with a thin rain falling from time to time.

Bonnie didn't care. There was her mother, older and tired with new lines in her face, the sad eyes a little sadder, but alive and well. All during the hours in the field, Bonnie would turn impulsively to the slender woman and embrace her, whisper endearments, cry against her withered cheek.

And there were the others. Bonnie's sister, younger and proud of her sister's exploits. "Here you are, Bonnie. We been cuttin' and pastin' everythin' about you. We even got that picture the paper printed of y'all with that Ranger fella."

And the children, to sing and play with, to take joy from. And the uncles and aunts, the cousins. And always Bonnie's mother, quiet and dignified, eyes a little regretful behind steel-rimmed glasses, hands veined and freckled, clasped tightly, too tightly, at her waist.

And, too soon it was time to go, Clyde said. Bonnie bit her lip and looked at him imploringly.

"A while longer, Clyde?"

He shook his head. "It's been too long, now honey. Too chancey."

She nodded and embraced her mother. "Oh, Mama, it was so fine to see you again. You look just wonderful. You take care of yourself, hear!"

Bonnie's mother stepped back and studied her daughter. Her glance went to Clyde, unblinking and with an awful calm that Clyde found disturbing.

"Clyde Barrow," she said without emphasis. "Bonnie was always a wild child, but everthin' she did wasn't bad, not by a jugful. Maybe *you* know the way with her. But I read about y'all in the papers and I'm just scared."

"Oh, Mama . . ."

"I know I'm just an old woman and I don't know nothin', and young folks ain't goin' to pay no mind . . ."

Clyde gave her a reassuring smile. "Mrs. Parker, don't believe what you read in them newspapers. Why, if we done half that stuff they write about we'd be millionaires. This ain't no play game for us. It's business, Mother Parker. You know hard times is on us, and this is the way we know best to make money."

"I understand what you're sayin', Clyde . . ."

He went on. "I wouldn't risk Bonnie just to make some money. So you don't worry your mind about it any more. Why, one time I knowed of a job where we could've made two thousand dollars easy, but I saw the law outside and I knew there'd be shootin' and I said to myself, 'Why, Bonnie could get hurt in there.' So I just drove right on by and let all that money lay."

"Well, I do worry."

Bonnie hugged her mother. "Oh, Mama, you don't want to do that. It's like Clyde says—he takes care of me good."

'We'll be quittin' this just as soon as the hard times are over," Clyde said encouragingly. "I can tell you that. Why, me and Bonnie were just talkin' the other day and we talked about when we'd settle down and get us a home."

"And I tol' Clyde," Bonnie said. "I tol' him I couldn't bear to live more'n three miles away from my precious mama."

Mrs Parker stared at her daughter with no change of expression. "No, you won't. You do that, Bonnie Parker, and you'll be sure enough killed dead by the law in twenty-four hours. So you just keep movin', runnin', for as long as you can. Yes sir, that's what you better do."

No one said anything as the old lady shuffled away. Nor

did either of them notice that it had begun to rain again. Harder this time.

Days ran into days and weeks into weeks and the Barrow gang discovered no resting place and what money they had went quickly, the price of life acutely inflated to those on the run. They slept where they could, ate where they felt safest. On this day, Clyde drew up in front of a hamburger joint.

"Okay, Buck," he said. "You and C. W. go to work this time."

"Right, baby brother."

There were only a few people inside and a lone short order cook to prepare food. "What's it goin' to be, mister?" he said to Buck.

"Lemme have five burgers, three beers and a couple of Cokes."

When the order was ready, the counterman arranged it carefully on some paper plates, covered them neatly with napkins, and slid them across the counter to Buck. He looked up, smiling, to collect his payment. The smile faded swiftly when he discovered a pistol pointed at his head.

"This is a stickup," Buck said easily.

It was then that C. W. stepped into the doorway, a double-barreled shotgun in his hands, a friendly smile on his little mouth, his tiny eyes quick and hard.

"I'll take all the cash you have in that cash register," Buck said.

The counterman handed it over without protest and Buck backed off toward the door. Suddenly he stopped.

"Say," he said, "what kind of fried pies you got today?"

The counterman's response was professionally polite, an automatic reaction. "Apricot, apple, and peach."

Buck considered that. "Reckon I'll have two apricot and three apple."

The food in hand, Buck backed out, C. W. covering his retreat, then following, running for the car.

A moment later the counterman burst out, yelling, "Help! Help! Somebody get the police!"

C. W. swung back bringing the shotgun to bear. His finger pressed down on the trigger. The force of the blast knocked the counterman straight up and off the ground, hurling him backward through the plate-glass window of his restaurant. C. W. waited until the sound of shattered glass had quieted before getting into the car.

Clyde drove slowly through a quiet residential neighborhood. Here the streets were lined with trees and the houses substantial, a place where people never broke the law, never concerned themselves with the police or guns, never worried about money. Bonnie thought that it would be nice to live in such a neighborhood. At the same time, a sense of uneasiness came over her. They should have been on some back road speeding away from that burger joint, putting distance between themselves and the inevitable pursuit. Clyde seemed particularly unconcerned, gazing out the window, enjoying the warm spring night, as if they were all out for a little sociable drive.

"Clyde," she said.

"Huh?"

"Don't you reckon we ought to be out on the road somewheres, gettin' out of this county, at least?"

"Sure. After a while."

"What are we waitin' for?" Buck put in.

"I figure this car is too well-known by now," Clyde explained, still searching the street. "It's time we got ourselves another one, one not identified to us."

C. W. agreed. "That's a good idea, Clyde. And lookee there, up ahead. There's two good-lookin' machines in front of that there house."

Clyde drew up behind the first car and killed the motor. He led the way out, looked over each of the cars, one a coupé the other a sedan.

"This one, I reckon," he said, indicating the sedan.

"It oughta be able to get up a good speed," C. W. said. "Specially after I get to work on the engine."

"Let's get in," Clyde ordered.

Eugene Grizzard was a round-faced man of no particular distinction. His smile was quick and fleeting, and his eyes were never still for very long. He explained that by saying that he was interested in seeing everything. But at this particular moment Eugene had eyes only for Velma Davis, his fiancé.

They were seated in the swing on the porch of Velma's parent's house, locked in each other's arms. Eugene approved of Velma. True she was twenty-eight, a little old to be unmarried, but he didn't care. She suited him. She had a kind face and a firm slender body which he had been allowed to explore with greater freedom recently. Not that Velma was a loose woman. Not a bit. She was good, one hundred percent, and would make him a wonderful wife, the kind of wife a man in his position needed.

He kissed her now and her lips quivered under his and parted slightly. His hand stroked her side, came to rest under her armpit, his thumb touching the soft swell of her breast. A highly stimulating experience, Eugene told himself. He moved his hand. Just a little.

"Oh, Eugene," Velma breathed. "Oh, now ... now, dear ..."

"Sweet thing ... so sweet ...'

"Eugene, I really shouldn't let you. Not yet. Not until we're husband and wife in the sight of man and God ..."

"That'll be soon enough," he husked, shifting closer, bending over her, nuzzling her neck.

She giggled and looked past his ear to the street. She watched with mild interest as the other car drew up behind her daddy's coupé. Who could that be, coming home at this hour? she wondered idly. Was it Laura McCandless, out cutting up again with that Fredricks fellow? She saw the people get out of their car and decided they were strangers. She watched as they strolled past the coupé and stood looking at Eugene's car, then got inside as if it were their own. Velma pushed Eugene's hand away.

"Aww, Velma," he protested.

"Say, Eugene, isn't that your car?"

His head turned. "Sure." The car began to move away from the curb, picking up speed. Eugene leaped to his feet. "Hey! That's my car! Hey!"

Eugene hurdled the railing edging the porch, went sprinting into the street, yelling after his fast disappearing car, shaking his fist in anger. Velma came up behind him.

"What are you going to do, sweetheart?" she said.

"Go after them. C'mon, we'll use your father's car."

"But . . ." she protested.

He cut her short. "You drive!"

She drove well, hands firm on the wheel, in total control of the speeding coupé and of herself. "We're gaining on them, Eugene. There they are, up ahead."

"Go faster," he urged. "Those punks! Wait'll I get my hands on them."

"What are you going to do, Eugene?"

"I'll tear 'em apart! Steal a man's car right from under him. I'll smash every one of them."

"You're very brave, Eugene."

"When I get my hands on those kids, Velma . . . I'll show them. I'll really teach them a lesson."

They were no more than fifty feet behind the other car now and gaining. Eugene urged her to greater speed.

"Force them off the road, Velma, and I'll give them something they deserve, a sound thrashing."

"What if they have guns?" she mused aloud.

His eyes swung violently from side to side and a brief smile lifted the corners of his mouth. He paled. "You know what I think, Velma?"

"What, Eugene?"

"That it wouldn't be fair, me beating up on those kids. We better get the police and let them handle this."

"All right, sweetheart."

"Turn around and head back to town. We'll go get the sheriff."

"All right."

"Well, turn around," he said peevishly.

She did so.

Up ahead, in Eugene's sedan, Buck had been watching through the rear window. He chuckled contentedly. "They stopped chasin' us," he said, twisting around, making himself comfortable. "They turned around."

"Oh, that's too bad," Clyde said mischievously. He thought for a moment. "Let's go take 'em!"

Clyde executed a U-turn in one swift, smooth maneuver, stomped down hard on the gas pedal. The distance between the two cars began to shrink at once.

In the coupé, Velma peered into the rear-view mirror. Her eyes widened. "Oh, my God, Eugene. They're coming after us."

He looked back. "Step on it, Velma," he shot out, a rising panic in his voice. "Step on it!"

"They're gaining on us," Velma said.

"Go faster! Go faster!"

"I've got the accelerator on the floor now. It won't go faster."

"What are we going to do, Velma? I mean, if they catch us, and they have guns, I mean."

The sedan came up alongside, kept pace, while the members of the Barrow gang looked in on Velma and Eugene, who carefully kept their eyes on the road in front of them. Abruptly, Clyde pulled ahead, forced the coupé over to the side. Both cars screeched to a halt.

Eugene and Velma watched as Clyde and the others got out and strolled back toward them. Terrified, Eugene rolled up his window, indicating Velma was to do likewise.

A menacing sight. Pressed around the coupé, faces distorted against the windows and the windshield, were five people, grinning madly, brandishing weapons. Clyde pointed a pistol at Eugene and made an exaggerated motion of shooting. Eugene blanched. Clyde grinned, and his friends laughed, and Eugene managed a wan smile himself. It disappeared quickly.

Clyde gestured with his pistol. 'C'mon, get out!" Neither Velma nor Eugene moved. "Get out, I said."

"What are we going to do, Eugene?" Velma asked.

"Do?" He looked at her in disbelief. "Why, we're going to get out of the car."

They came out, hands raised and shaking.

"Hello," Eugene said. "Hello, everybody. Hello. Hello."

C. W. smiled. "Howdo, folks."

"What are we goin' to do with 'em?" Buck asked.

Clyde considered the question. "Let's take 'em along." He pointed to the sedan with his pistol. "Get in there."

Eugene's car was crowded. Clyde drove and Bonnie sat next to him, C. W. alongside her. Buck, Blanche, Eugene, and Velma were jammed into the back seat. To make matters more uncomfortable, the road they were on was rough, unpaved, sliced with ruts and potholes. But neither Eugene nor Velma was prepared to object. As for Clyde and his friends, they were pleased to have some company, different faces, people from another world who could talk about other things, introduce a diversion however temporary and brief.

"What's your names?" Buck said.

"I'm Eugene Grizzard."

"I'm Velma Davis."

"Well, howdy," Buck said. "We're the Barrow gang. That there is Clyde drivin' and I'm Buck."

The blood drained out of Eugene's cheeks and he and Velma clutched desperately at each other.

"Look," Bonnie said warmly. "Don't be scared, folks.

It ain't like you was the law. You're just folks like us."

Eugene saw a ray of hope. "Yeah," he said. "Yeah, that's the truth. Just folks."

"I expect you been readin' about us," Clyde said over his shoulder. "In the newspapers."

They answered simultaneously. "Yes," Eugene said.

"No," Velma said.

They glared at each other.

Eugene spoke with emphasis. He was sure he knew the proper strategy to save themselves from this mad crew. "*Yes,*" he said. "Yes, we have, too, been reading about them, Velma."

Bonnie laughed at the confusion. "Well, you two must be in love, I bet."

Eugene lowered his eyes and nodded shyly, then more vigorously.

Buck clapped him on the back. "Well, now, boy, when you gonna marry the girl?"

They all laughed at that and the tensions began to wash away. They drove on and as time passed a feeling of comradeship was born. Buck began telling jokes, building up to his favorite.

"So then she drinks her milk down again every drop. And she looks over at her son and says, 'Son, whatever you do, *don't sell that cow!*'"

Eugene laughed loudly and Velma joined in. From the others, there was only silence; they had heard Buck tell the story too many times before.

Bonnie wanted to keep Buck quiet. She turned to Velma, smiling in a friendly fashion. "How old are you, honey?"

"Thirty-three," Velma answered without thinking. She stiffened. There was no missing the look of surprise and dismay on Eugene's face. Velma knew she had committed a serious error.

Later, they stopped at a roadside diner and Velma and Bonnie brought out their dinner—sandwiches, drinks, side orders of French fries. They ate in the car, almost a family picnic, light and airy, a sense of belonging, a private society hurtling through the black night.

"Now, let's see," Velma said. "I ordered some French fries, didn't I?"

Buck passed them along. "Here you go."

"Take it easy on those French fries, Velma," Clyde warned gaily. "Ain't that right, Eugene?"

Eugene studied his hamburger. "This isn't mine," he said finally, a note of annoyance in his voice. "I ordered mine well done. Now who's got my hamburger?"

C. W., his mouth stuffed, checked the burger in his fist. "Oh," he muttered thickly. "Is this supposed to be yours?" He extended the half-eaten burger in Eugene's direction.

Eugene viewed it with distaste. "That's okay. Forget it." Clyde laughed at Eugene's discomfort.

Buck, chewing his food with animal vigor, guffawed loudly. "I sure am havin' me a good time!"

"Me too," Blanche said.

"How about you folks?" Buck said to Eugene.

"Sure am. Best time I ever had."

"Me, too," Velma said.

"Ain't you glad we picked you up?" Buck said.

"Sure," Eugene said. "This is the best time I had in years. Honest."

Clyde chuckled. "Hey, maybe y'all ought to join up with us, become members of the Barrow gang."

That drew a delighted sound out of Eugene. "Ha! Wouldn't they be surprised back home to hear that? Eugene Grizzard a part of the notorious Barrow gang!"

Velma giggled with pleasure at the thought. "Imagine! What would Martha and Bill say if they heard that?" Her laughter came in waves, each shriller and louder.

"Oh, God!" Eugene gasped, tears beginning to stream out of his eyes. "They'd throw a fit! Me, doing that!"

"What do you *do*, anyway?" Bonnie put in, laughing.

Eugene fought for breath, his laugh fading. "I'm an undertaker." he said.

The inside of the car went quiet, an ominous stillness. For a long interval no one spoke. Only the sound of their breathing was audible. It was Bonnie, taut, anxious, speaking from between clenched teeth, who said it for them all.

"Get them out of here."

12

Run.

That's all they seemed to do, speeding from one place to another, and always there was an invisible cloud pressing down, stirring them to some dim awareness of what lay ahead. And what lay ahead was being shaped by what they left behind, a trail of robberies and killings, of outraged citizenry too happy to report their whereabouts to the police, their names and faces as familiar as movie star's.

Bonnie and Clyde. First billing was always theirs. And the small but known supporting cast. Buck and Blanche. Plus a third, unidentified man.

Behind them also was a tall Texas Ranger, bitter and dedicated, a man with a committed glitter in his far-seeing eyes, a man whose handlebar mustache gave him the look of an avenger who would not be denied. A man tormented, unable to live with mockery. A man yearning to repay those who had made of him a laughingstock before the inhabitants of his special world. So he came on, after them, asking questions, phoning ahead, checking local police, bus stops, motor courts, roadside diners. Wherever they might have paused to rest or refresh themselves. And no matter where they went, he learned of it and came after them.

They felt safe enough in Platte City, Iowa, a town not too different from so many others they had seen and passed through. It was a still place, life moving at a measured pace, and little ever happened to excite the citizens. Or the police force. Least of all, nothing like the Barrow gang. Bank robberies and killings were events to plague other towns. Here, in the heartland of America, people went from day to day knowing what to expect of their lives, of their neighbors, and a man marked only the truly important days, like the Fourth of July and Christmas and Thanksgiving. The days that mattered.

It would have upset Platte City to have learned that Clyde Barrow and his friends had checked into the Platte City Motel, had rented adjoining cabins with connected garages. Platte City didn't want people like Clyde Barrow around and would have taken suitable action had his presence become public knowledge. But on this day no one knew. Not yet.

They all gathered in one of the cabins. Buck lounged in one of the overstuffed chairs, Blanche in another just across from him, Clyde and C. W. sprawled across the double bed, each lost in his own thoughts. And Bonnie paced the room. There was a special quality to her movements, a feline thing, fluid and reaching, as if all her forces, emotional and intellectual, were gathering in one place, a tight fusing of all needs and desires, a tightening band that stretched almost beyond tolerance.

She stopped, gazed balefully around. "What is this, a public room?"

No one replied and she swore tightly. She pointed at Buck and Blanche. "You two got your own room, why don't you go there? Stay there. By yourselves."

Clyde sighed and heaved himself off the bed. "Relax, honey, don't be so jumpy. Here. Why'n't you lay down and take it easy? I reckon we're all a little testy."

Buck looked lazily at Bonnie who had remained standing in the middle of the room. "What's botherin' her?" His normal good humor was absent. "What's botherin' her?" he said, directing himself to Clyde this time.

Clyde turned away. He wanted to avoid any arguments. They had all been together too long and he wished they could separate, at least for a while. That was worth some hard thinking, to figure a way. "Lay off, Buck," he said mildly.

Buck wasn't having any of that. His nerves were rubbed raw. Blanche had been at him almost constantly to leave Clyde, to go and live with her daddy, to join him in the church. Shoot! That wasn't for Buck Barrow. But not this either, this hanging around doing nothing, cooped up in tiny cabin rooms, always hiding from the police. And that Bonnie! She was okay except that sometimes she got to feeling too big for her britches. Face it, Buck told himself, she was only Clyde's girl, not even properly married and all. He snorted disparagingly and jerked his head in her direction.

"What's botherin' her?" he repeated harshly.

"Ain't nothin' the matter with me," Bonnie snapped off. "Nothin' that bein' away from you and that wife of yours wouldn't fix in a big hurry."

Buck straightened up. "Now lookee here . . ."

"You can't talk about me that way," Blanche objected. "I ain't a piece of dirt or something!"

"That's exactly what you are," Bonnie shot back.

Clyde felt he had to speak up before the situation got out of hand. He turned to Bonnie. "C'mon, try to be a little more sociable."

"You can go to hell!"

"Listen, Bonnie . . ."

"Don't you tell me what to do, Clyde Barrow."

"Well, damn!" Clyde said. "Well, dammit it all to hell! You can both go jump in the lake, both of you."

He swung away, striding over to the far wall, pressing his forehead against the cheap wallpaper with all his strength, the veins in his neck bulging. He counted silently to ten, and ten more. The resentment oozed out of him and he went over to Bonnie and tried to kiss her. She turned her face.

He grinned, that boyish grin that always stirred her, made her want to embrace him and pet him and hold him against her bosom. She ignored him. He put his thumbs in his ears and made a silly face, crossing his eyes, waggling his fingers, his tongue popping in and out of his mouth like some idiot marionette gone beserk.

She glared at him. "Stop it, Clyde. Let me alone. Just don't bother me, hear!"

He swallowed an angry retort and swung away. The silence was oppressively thick and worrisome. It was C. W. who shattered the mounting tension. He sat up and stretched, yawning noisily, almost oblivious to what had been happening.

"Boy," he said, "I'm about to starve to death. Ain't anybody else hungry?"

There were affirmative murmurs from the others.

"That's a good idea," Clyde agreed hurriedly. "I saw a chicken place a few miles back. Who all wants to go get some food?"

Blanche stood up, head held proud and defiant. "I will. I'm sure gettin' plenty tired of sittin' around here and lookin' at your long faces anyway."

"You can't drive, honey-love," Buck said. He made no move to get out of his chair.

"That ain't all she can't do," Bonnie muttered.

"Now look here," Blanche began.

"I'll go with you, Blanche," C. W. said without enthusiasm. "I'll drive for you."

"That's mighty nice of you, C. W.," Buck said.

"What's everybody want?" C. W. asked.

"What d'you reckon they got?" Buck asked thoughtfully.

Clyde said, "Just five chicken dinners. That's all."

106

"And somethin' for dessert," Buck added, grinning. C. W. looked at Clyde, who nodded.

"See if they got peach ice cream," Buck said. He patted his bulging paunch lovingly.

"Don't worry, lover," Blanche said. "I'll find you some ice cream. I'm goin' to take good care of my man."

Bonnie snorted in disgust and turned away. The door closed signaling the departure of Blanche and C. W. All at once a sense of loss came over Bonnie and she was afraid she was going to cry. She walked swiftly into the other room, slamming the door, dropping onto the bed, kicking off her shoes, rolling onto her stomach, trying not to think, not to feel, making her brain a black void, willing herself to sleep. It refused to come and she pounded her fist against the mattress in frustration.

Her mind reached back to her room in her mother's house. It was no different now, the same sense of being restricted, caged, unable to breath, a grounded bird, her wings clipped. She wanted . . . oh, how she wanted. But . . . what?

"Baby, what's wrong?"

She rolled over. Clyde was standing there looking down at her, that worried crease between his eyes. She stretched out her arms and he came to her. His body was strong, well-muscled, and the weight of him on her was deeply stimulating. She held him tightly and her middle reached, rolled, and twisted, and her lips parted and went up to his. The kiss was long, warm, penetrating, different in some unnamed way than ever before.

Her arms tightened and one hand slid down the small of his back onto his tight flat bottom and she moved against him with a driving insistence and he responded as he never had before. She guided his hand to her breast. His fingers were strong but gentle and a starburst of sensation stirred just under her nipple and spread swiftly, a churning emotional pool traveling along the length of her to that private place which she longed to offer to Clyde. He lifted his mouth away from her.

"Listen," he murmured.

"Hush, now. Just kiss me again."

"You know how I feel . . ."

She placed her hands carefully, one on each side of his face, and reached up for his mouth again, found it and after a brief interlude, let her tongue caress his lips, circling the oval of his mouth, touching the backs of his teeth, dancing along the hard ridge of gumline, finding the sensitive inner cheek. A soft moan sounded back in his throat and he rolled onto his back. She went after him.

"We shouldn't be doin' this," he said. "It ain't proper."

"I love you, Clyde."

"And me you, Bonnie. Still that don't mean we got the right to be rutting aroun' like a couple of hounds in heat."

She grinned and her fingers traced the line of his jaw. "Maybe those dogs know something without us tellin' them. . . ."

A silent struggle was going on within, and she could see it. He shoved himself erect, turning abruptly away. "This ain't right."

"It is, Clyde. As right as anything could be."

A spasm coursed through his strong body. He went to the far wall.

"You don't understand," he said, after a silent minute.

"I love you, Clyde. Isn't that enough?"

He filled his lungs with air and tried to close his mind. A thousand different thoughts skittered around inside his skull, memories that were best forgotten, pictures evil and disturbing. There was one single, recurrent image. His father and mother, together naked in bed, bodies straining and thrusting, his father pounding his mother hard and painfully. The sounds, the pitiful plaints of a woman soft and vulnerable, the pain, the indignity, the violence done, and later the recriminations, the talk of failure, of the closeness of something dear but never fulfilled, of repeated experiences that left her empty and yearning for what never was.

Clyde had vowed, long before he knew what it was he was vowing, long before he could understand, that he would never pain a woman, never fail to provide what a woman he loved wanted. And to insure that he would never fail, it came to his mind that there were things best left undone.

There had been a girl when he was sixteen. She had been older by two years, years larded with experience and knowledge. And she had taken him behind the sports field in back of the grade school and taught him how to kiss, how to caress a girl, and the excitement in him had swelled and become unbearable until he wanted to scream. Then she had made those sounds, small pitiful sounds deep in her throat and her body had writhed under him as if in protest and he knew, knew, *knew* that he was causing her pain. He had twisted away, distraught, edgy, almost angry, stood up, ignoring the plaintive look in her eyes, averting his face so he could not see her spread legs and her pale white belly and the shadowed wedge that drew him and repelled him at the same time. She had spoken his name once, low and pleading, and he had pivoted away, alternately walking and running all the way home. And was safe.

"Clyde!"

He grunted but could not face Bonnie. He loved her too much to do her any harm, any injury.

"Clyde, come back to me."

"You don't know what you're sayin'."

"I love you and I want you, Clyde."

"I can't. We mustn't."

There was the sound of the bed creaking and her footsteps, a soft padding, and he sensed her at his shoulder though she made no effort to touch him.

"It's been a long time since that first day, Clyde. Remember? I was standing at the window lookin' out thinkin' I was about to go out of my mind when I looked down and there you was about to steal Mama's car. You remember?"

"I remember,"

"You remember how I looked to you that minute, that exact minute?"

He exhaled silently. "I remember."

"Tell me."

"There ain't nothin' to tell."

"*Tell* me."

He swallowed. "You weren't wearin' clothes. Nothin' at all."

"Was I pretty to you, Clyde?"

"You were beautiful."

"Tell me."

"I was able to see your breasts."

"And . . .?"

"You were . . . beautiful. . . ."

"I haven't changed, Clyde." He made no answer, held himself very stiffly. "Wouldn't you want to see me again? Now? Close up, Clyde? Very close?"

Her hand came to rest on his shoulder and moved lower, fingers caressing his spine. She lay her cheek against his back.

"I love you, Clyde."

It was building in him, desire, the need, the ache to hold her, to feel her softness against his own flesh, to taste her mouth. Clumsily, unsure, he swung around and their mouths closed on each other.

When they broke she was fighting for air and laughing.

"C'mon," she said. "C'mon."

"Where?"

She had his hand in hers and was tugging. "This way, sweetheart, this way, to the bed."

He held back. "Bonnie . . . I'm afraid."

"Me too," she laughed. "Me too. We'll be afraid together and whip our fear together."

He wet his mouth and allowed her to lead him. She sat

on the edge of the bed and began to unbutton his shirt. Her mouth found his naked chest, lips working, moist and warm, and her tongue a blazing probe. Her hands fumbled with his belt.

"Bonnie, I don't want to hurt you."

"Oh, my darlin' love. You ain't never goin' to hurt me, not a single solitary time."

"How can you know?"

She smiled and brushed at his hair. "I *know*."

He knelt and they kissed, sweet and lingering. Gradually, a slow ascent beginning somewhere behind his navel, a climb to peaks never before known and there was a tingling on his skin as if a thousand dancing flowers skipped their way up and down his limbs, along his torso. He shivered in delight. In anticipation. In fear.

She was undressing him, fingers unhurried and certain, steady, so as not to give alarm. He stood naked and wanted to conceal himself, to hide from her view, but she held him and soothed him and loved his flesh and brought it back to life and shored up his manhood, keeping his passion vibrant and strong.

After a while, she stripped off her own clothing, rapidly, afraid to be apart from him for too long. Then they were together, mouth to mouth, breast to breast, belly to belly, arms and legs entwined, hands reaching with curiosity and affection.

"Oh, Bonnie, I never knew ..."

"Let me show you, darling. ..."

"That way?"

"Oh, yes, my love. That way. And here, here, too, like that. Oh, perfect."

"It's almost too ... much. ..."

"Too much and not enough ..."

Her body arched and strained upward against him and he worked against her flesh, forcing her back onto the mattress. It was all thick emotion and feeling, spreading into the furthest reaches of every limb, seeping into vital organs, a quickening tempo that throbbed deeply and sent the blood pounding behind their eyes. A pendulous quality to it all, a heavy, demanding, insistent thing that would no longer be denied, that made itself known erupting from a dark secret place in him, a distant shadowy melody with its singular rhythms and harmonies. All was reaching and taking, and finding certain hollows, moist and mysterious, giving, getting, a thumping, at once gentle and savage, unlearnable except in this school.

"Bonnie! . . ."

"My darlin' . . ."

"I love you!"

"I love you!"

"Bonnie!"

"Oh, yes . . ."

"I can't . . ."

"Oh, no. Don't. Don't wait. No waitin'. Just . . . give . . . me. Give . . . me . . . everythin'. Give . . . splash me . . . all . . . you. Give . . . give . . . oh, yes, baby, give . . . to . . . me . . ."

He screamed into her mouth.

He stood by the window and gazed sightlessly into the bright daylight. A warm flood seemed to break over him in slow, successive waves, and he allowed it to happen.

"Bonnie," he said quietly, not turning.

"Hmmm."

She lay naked under the sheet, curled and twisted hair thick and female over her face, breasts heavy, all woman. Content. Full.

A long stride took him alongside the bed. He spread his hands helplessly. "Was it . . . right? I mean, *right*."

"You're beautiful."

A boyish agitation filled his mouth and made him stutter. "No. I mean, *right*. It's important that it be right. I mean, you have to tell me so I can know and learn for you. It's important."

She came up on one elbow and a lazy smile bent her mouth. Lidded eyes swam into focus. "No woman ever had a man so *right*. The *rightest*."

"You've got to tell me."

She held out her arms. "Come and I will."

And this time he didn't have to ask.

13

"THIS SURE is nice."

Blanche glanced sidelong at C. W. at the wheel of the car and turned away. She took a last drag on her cigarette, tossed the butt out of the window.

"I mean, us ridin' along together this way. We never did get much time to talk," C. W. went on, his manner open, friendly. "Things I heard you say to Buck or Clyde, I figured we got a whole lot in common."

Blanche shifted around in her seat and stared at the little round man. Maybe he was right. Maybe they did have a lot in common. He wasn't like Clyde, so tough and distant. Or Bonnie, mean and cold.

"How do you mean, in common?" she said cautiously.

C. W. shrugged. "Don't know. Just tryin' to be friendly, that's all."

She was vaguely disappointed. She needed a friend, someone to talk to, share her concerns with, someone who would understand. Sudden irritation with C. W. flashed through her.

"Slow down, willya?" she barked.

"I'm only doin' forty-five."

Tension had been mounting in Blanche and it seemed

worse today, a swelling pressure that allowed her no peace. She lit another cigarette and puffed anxiously.

C. W. smiled at her. "You sure are smokin' all the time lately."

"So what?"

"Nothin'."

"Oh, God. . . ." Blanche let her head drop into her hand and a sad sigh came out of her. She closed her eyes and tried not to think, to forget where she was, what had been happening to her.

C. W. looked at her. After a moment, he directed his attention back to the road. A bright look came into his little eyes, the look of discovery. C. W. had had an idea.

"Hey! Blanche!"

She made a small sound but didn't move.

"I got an idea."

"Yeah?" she said wearily.

"Whyn't you go back home to your papa?"

Her head came up and she gazed at C. W. with new interest. "Oh, C. W., if only I could," she burst out. "If I could just do that one thing! Oh, there's no tellin' why this all happened." She shifted around so that she faced him directly. "Did I ever tell you that I was a preacher's daughter?"

"Well, how about that! I never knew that."

She shook her head vigorously. "Well, it is a fact, an ab-so-lute true fact."

A smile curved C. W.'s mouth and remained there. "Hey!" he said, after a while. "What church is your papa affiliated with?"

"Baptist, of course." She puffed on the cigarette. "Oh, and he thought the world of Buck, my daddy did, even knowing that Buck was serving in jail. That's the kind of man my daddy was. He forgive him for that 'cause he paid his debt to society."

"We were Disciples of Christ."

"I mean, that's the Christian way. Forgiveness and love, an' all."

The car swung to the right and stopped. C. W. turned off the engine and looked at Blanche patiently.

"Why'd you stop?" she asked.

"We're here, the chicken café."

"Oh," she said. Then, with irritation: "Well, let's go inside."

The restaurant was long and narrow, a wooden counter running its length. Only a few people were at the counter when C. W. and Blanche entered, one of them a lean sheriff's deputy in dusty khaki's. He glanced up automatically at their appearance but showed no further interest and went back to his food. Blanche went over to the take-out counter and put in her order, fiddling nervously with her purse while she waited. C. W. stood a few feet away, oblivious of his surroundings, lost in some world of his own making.

"Here y'are, ma'am." It was the counterman, extending a brown paper bag containing Blanche's order. She searched through her purse.

"Hey, C. W.," she said, voice brassy and insistent. "I ain't got my money. Give me some, willya?"

The deputy looked over without lifting his head, chewing methodically. Women! he thought wryly, watching the byplay.

C. W. opened his jacket in order to get to his back pocket and his money. The deputy stopped eating. There was no mistaking the black butt of a .38 pistol jutting up out of C. W.'s pants. The deputy lowered his eyes. When he heard C. W. and Blanche leave, he looked up.

"Charley!" he called to the counterman.

"Yeah?"

"Get on that telephone of yours. I want to talk to Sheriff Smoot. And I mean, right now."

The chicken dinners helped. The food satisfied their hunger and helped calm jangled nerves. By the time night came on, they were ready for bed. All but Bonnie and Clyde. There was a new kind of excitement in each of them, a continuing high note of energy and anticipation that refused to be stilled.

Only the soft glow of the lone bedlamp illuminated their bedroom. Bonnie was on the bed in her nightdress, her knees drawn under her chin, smoking, concentrating hard. Clyde reclined next to her in his undershorts, head resting in his hand, a cigarette drooping out of the corner of his mouth, squinting against the plume of smoke.

"Go ahead," he urged softly.

"Wait a minute. I'm thinkin'." She closed her eyes tightly. After a beat or two, they rolled open, a mischievous glint in them. "*T*" she said.

He considered that. "*U*."

"*T . . . U . . .*' She hesitated, then, triumphantly: "*X!*"

"Tux . . . er, now wait a sec . . . S!"

A puzzled expression faded onto Bonnie's face. "Tuxs? I challenge you!"

"Tuxedo."

A derisive laugh erupted out of her. "*Tuxedo!* There ain't no *S* in tuxedo."

"Damn!"

She laughed again, a light happy sound. "You lose again! That's three in a row! That makes you half a ghost, and I ain't any part of a ghost yet."

"Oh, yeah," he said playfully. "Only you look like one, though. You ain't got no meat left on your ribs."

With that he launched himself at her, fingers massaging her ribs. A rising whoop of laughter leaped out of her and her body arched as she tried to twist away from him.

"Stop, Clyde! Stop! Clyde, stop. Clyde!"

He kept at her and they thrashed around on the bed, limbs entwined, laughing wildly. Soon she was tickling him and for them both there was a new freedom, this physical thing between them, so warm and personal, so innocent and intimate. A new thing, strange still, but growing.

"Hey, now! Will you two just shut up? Can't I get some sleep, darn it?" It was C. W., sitting up in his place in the big chair across the room.

His words had no impact on Bonnie and Clyde. They continued to giggle, to roll around on the bed. C. W. snorted in disgust and got out of the chair, taking his pillow.

"A man can't get any rest around here," he complained. "I am goin' to sleep out in the car where I can get some peace and quiet."

He reached for the blanket, letting it drag along the floor behind him, shuffled toward the door connecting the room with the garage. As he passed in front of the window, it was filled with a great, blinding light. C. W. blinked and fell back.

"What the hell . . . !"

Clyde sat upright. No longer was he laughing. He reached for his pants. "It's the law!"

The alert deputy at the chicken café had done his job well. A few questions around town, visits paid to this motor court, that rooming house, until by a process of elimination the right one was located. And now this.

Six police cars were ranged across the lawn outside the cabins occupied by the Barrow gang, the cars crowded with armed police officers. Four of them advanced across the expanse of grass, guns ready, walking with the cautious stiffness so natural to men crowding close to death. They edged up to the cabin in which Buck and Blanche slept. One of them knocked loudly.

"Open up, this is the police!"

Buck and Blanche sat upright in bed. He reached for his gun, about to throw the challenge back at them. Blanche's hand shot out, clamped over his mouth before he could speak.

"The men are on the other side!" she called out.

It worked. The four lawmen edged their way across the lawn, past the connected garages, toward Clyde and Bonnie's cabin. They were no more than twenty feet from the cabin door, when the brittle crash of a breaking window alerted them.

"Watch out!" came the warning cry.

It was too late. Blasts of gunfire broke open the night and one officer went tumbling to the ground. The others ran for cover.

Inside, C. W. and Bonnie were at the windows, firing steadily at the police cars, at the lawmen scattering into position.

"We got to get out of here!" Clyde shouted. "That's our only chance! I'm goin' in after the car!"

"Okay!" Bonnie called, still firing. Two lawmen fell to the ground and two more went racing for shelter. Out of the night, without warning, came a blinding light. She shielded her eyes.

"What the hell is that!" C. W. cried.

She tried desperately to see. "It's an armored car!" she yelled. "The bastards are using an armored car! Shoot it down, C. W.! Shoot it down!"

They began to fire, Bonnie blasting away with two pistols, C. W. using a Thompson submachine gun. The volley shattered the window of the armored car and the vehicle veered as the driver, badly wounded, slumped over the wheel. His body pressed down on the horn, sending an errie blast into the night air, blaring in counterpoint to the crackling gunfire.

In the garage, Clyde checked the Browning Automatic Rifle cradled in his arm before moving to the door, a door trembling under the impact of bullets breaking it apart. With one quick movement, he flung it open, triggering the automatic weapon at the same time, loosing a stream of bullets at the glaring lights outside. He ran back to the car and jumped in. One hand was on the steering wheel, the other on the BAR, shooting through the open window, as he drove the car into the driveway, the battle raging all around him.

Slugs whizzed past but he kept shooting back. The door of

the cabin flew open and Bonnie and C. W. came charging out, firing into the night. Crouching, they made it across the open space and into the car.

"Where's Buck and Blanche?" Bonnie cried.

"We goin' to leave them?" C. W. shouted.

"There!" Clyde yelled. "There they are! Keep shootin'!"

The door of the other cabin had opened and Buck and Blanche, holding a mattress in front of them for protection, inched out. With his free hand, Buck fired at the police.

"C'mon, Buck!" Clyde yelled. "This way!"

They tried to move faster, but the mattress was heavy and running was difficult. Bullets thudded into the mattress and one went on through and struck Buck. He screamed in pain and toppled over. Unable to hold up the mattress alone, Blanche fell too.

"Buck's hit!" Clyde cried. "I'm goin' after him!"

"You'll get killed!" Bonnie protested.

He was out of the car and running low and fast, slugs whistling past, digging up clumps of grass at his heels. In a single motion, Clyde heaved the mattress aside, grasped Buck under the arms, and headed back for the car. A hysterical Blanche followed, screaming.

"They shot Buck! They shot him!"

The volume of gunfire was deafening now and it seemed impossible that any of them could survive the intensive field of fire being layed down by the police. The car shuddered under the thud of slugs but somehow Clyde got the engine started and from a standing start the car leaped ahead like a crazed stallion, the speedometer swinging madly toward sixty before they were halfway down the driveway. A deputy appeared in their path with a double-barreled rifle.

He leaped aside at the last second, firing as he fell. One bullet hit the side window, shattering the glass into thousands of tiny slivers. Blanche fell back, screaming, hands over her face.

"I've been hit! I've been shot!"

A piece of glass had lodged in her eye. Something warm and

wet oozed up between her fingers and that set her to screaming again.

"I'm bleedin'! I'm goin' to bleed to death!"

No one paid any attention. They were too busy shooting at the squad cars that swung out in pursuit. The car careered crazily along the highway, Clyde fighting for control, his senses reeling, trying to understand what had happened, how the police had found them, at the same time struggling to think ahead, to find a way out.

He managed to put some distance between them and the trailing police and the shooting stopped. He crouched forward, clenching the wheel tightly, peering into the onrushing night, hunting an avenue of escape.

Around him, all was chaos and hysteria. Buck, bleeding from a terrible wound in his skull, tossed blindly about, moaning, crying out in anguish. Blanche, torn with her own pain as well as concern for her husband, sobbed and groaned, begged Clyde to take them to a hospital, to find a doctor.

"He's your brother," she muttered plaintively. "Help him. Please don't let Buck die."

C. W. sat among this misery and sobbed silently, the submachine gun cradled in his lap.

"Keep quiet!" Bonnie screamed. "All of you!"

No one listened to her.

"I think we've lost 'em," Clyde said.

Some thirty minutes had passed since they had begun their run. The inside of the car was comparatively still now, broken by only an occasional moan from Buck. Blanche held her face in her hands, rocking piously but making no sound.

"We can use another car," Clyde muttered. "Keep your eyes peeled."

They went speeding down a pleasant suburban street, past large, comfortable houses, nobody speaking.

"There!" Bonnie said finally. "On the right."

"C. W., you get it and follow me," Clyde ordered.

"Okay."

Clyde braked the car and C. W. got out, climbed into the other vehicle, a new and expensive touring car, backed it out of the driveway, and fell in behind Clyde. In tandem, they drove off.

C. W. lost track of time. Alone in the stolen limousine, he steered with one hand, crying all the time, muttering his fears, his confusion. He had never thought it would be this way, all the shooting, the killing, the pain and the blood. He hadn't meant it to be this way at all.

Neither had Clyde. All the fun had gone out of it long ago, all the glamor. Only the fear remained, the sense of being hunted, tracked down, being forced into some blind alley with no escape. His lungs burned and he yearned to lie under the high speckled sky and breathe fresh country air.

"We better stop somewhere," Bonnie said to him. "We got to rest." She glanced into the back seat. "Buck is hurt bad, Clyde. Real bad. And Blanche too."

He grunted. They were on a back road now and speeding past a row of high, leafy shadows. Swinging around a curve, he spotted a wide, flat field. It looked peaceful and quiet, a lush meadow surrounded by a ring of trees, a dense forest.

"Here," Clyde said. "We'll stop here."

The two cars swung into the field, headlights slicing through the dark, circling as if scouting the terrain, bouncing to a stop at last near the middle of the meadow. Slowly, reluctantly, almost, as it afraid to leave the somehow sanctified and secure confines of the cars, they staggered onto the grass, helping each other.

In the glare of the headlights, they were able to look at each other. Half-naked in pajamas, in nightgowns, in pants, glistening with sweat and blood. Dirty. Weary. Terror carved into faces so recently young.

Clyde and C. W. eased Buck out of the car and laid him on the thick grass. Clyde knelt and tried to do what he could for his brother. A single glance at the gaping wound in Buck's skull told him that for Buck there was nothing to be done.

Buck semiconscious, moaned and muttered something. Blanche sank to her knees, still clutching at her eyes, praying with mournful hysteria.

"Oh, dear God, please help us! Dear father in heaven, get us out of this and Buck will never do another bad thing in his life. I promise you, God, he'll be good ..."

Bonnie stood off to one side staring at the tableau. C. W. joined her. He gestured toward Buck.

"He ain't got a chance. Half his head is blown off."

"Shut up, C. W.," she said kindly.

It was then that Blanche screamed, the piercing lament of a stricken beast. "My eyes!" She screamed again. "God! I think I'm blind." She began to cry hysterically.

Bonnie went over to the car and came back with a pair of sunglasses. She put them on Blanche.

"You'll be all right, Blanche," she murmured.

"Please," Blanche cried. "Please, get us to a doctor. You got to. We'll die here."

Bonnie straightened up and her voice was edged with a tough realism. "Can't go to a doctor now. We've got to get out of this mess."

"Clyde," Blanche called. "Clyde, please get us to a doctor. We're goin' to die."

"I can't do that, Blanche," he said quietly. "It's just too dangerous."

"He's your brother!"

Clyde looked down at Buck. His mouth firmed up and he held himself very stiffly. "No. I ... can't ... do it."

Buck stirred and tried to sit up. "Brother, that you? Got to ... get a doctor ... get me a doctor ..." He fell back, unconscious.

Strange, high moans began to come out of Blanche as she swayed back and forth, praying.

C. W. lowered himself to the ground, his eyes closed, breathing in the sweet green scent of the meadow.

Bonnie sat on the running board of one of the cars and stared into the night.

Clyde remained at his brother's side, gently stroking his hair, waiting for him to die.

14

DAY CAME slowly. But when finally it did it was on them almost without notice. First the field grew lighter, a gray stillness, surrounded by the looming blackwall of the trees. And in the light, the two cars, the one ancient, scarred, as wounded as the people around it; the other, shiny new, rich and powerful.

The sky lightened and cast its brightness over the field. In the east, the sun swung up and drew the blackness of the trees into elongated shadows.

The Barrow gang gave no recognition to the new day. There was Blanche weeping without tears. Clyde still with Buck, cradling the torn head. C. W., hunkered down, plucking absently at the grass. There was Bonnie, standing and smoking, not allowing herself to think.

Quiet was everywhere.

All at once, a subtle movement at the far edge of the woods. A splash of whiteness against the black-green shadows. A man stepped into the open and formed a megaphone with his hands.

"Sur-render!"

It drifted to them like that, floating gently on the morning air, three loosely connected sounds. And it took time for it to register, for them to comprehend, to locate the source.

Then, frantic, scrambling movement. Scuttling for guns, the small ones, the pistols. Shooting off at the distant trees, at the man in the white shirt, a strange, luminous figure, some pastoral apparition. Abruptly gone. The shooting ceased, replaced by an extended silent interval.

The man. Had he really been there or was it some awful trick of their imaginations? Time held still.

"Let's get out of here!" Clyde shouted.

A ring of fire. Gunfire. Twinkling red and white puffs. From every bush, from behind every tree, every fallen log. A deadly stinging attack designed to destroy the Barrow gang for all time.

"We're surrounded!" C. W. yelled.

"There must be a couple of hundred of them!" Bonnie moaned.

She was right. The deputy in the chicken café had alerted the sheriff and he had alerted every peace officer in the vicinity, had mustered every farmer who owned a hunting rifle, every youth with a squirrel gun, every shopkeeer who had a shotgun. And each one of them wanted to be part of it, to be in on the kill, the death of Bonnie and Clyde, all of them. It was the kind of thing a man would be able to brag about for all his days, a truly important event. They poured lead into the center of the meadow in the name of law and order, each man and boy of them determined to do his part to keep the peace.

For Clyde, for the others, it was a bad dream, a nightmare, gray, misty, all movement in slow motion, a world gone mad and out of synchronization. Crouching, crawling, scrambling, tripping, falling, they headed for the nearest car, the old one, the one battle-scarred and trustworthy.

Escape was all there was. To stand and fight would have been insane, ludicrous, suicidal. Somehow they made it into the car, Clyde half-dragging Buck, partially revived, cursing and protesting, determined through his agony to live out his time in his own way.

Behind the wheel, Clyde jerked at the gearshift, stamped down on the gas pedal. The car lurched towards the woods and was met by a volley of shots. The car veered, bounced, a creature gone mad, toward a thick tree. A man appeared, rifle leveled. He squeezed off a shot. The windshield shattered.

The car spun off in another direction, performing an eccentric dance. It swerved and looped toward the wooded edges of the meadow and back to the center.

Clyde fought the wheel, steered for the far side of the field. Another man appeared. He snapped off a shot. Clyde swore and grabbed his left arm, blood appearing between his fingers.

The car, on its own, executed a wide slow arc, out of control, bulling its way across the field, smashing finally into a tree stump. It wheezed and groaned and the motor went dead, a headlight drooped and a fender fell off.

The old car was finished.

But not the Barrow gang. Out there in the morning sunlight, bright and gleaming, emanating power and speed, waited the other car.

"C'mon," Clyde said, leading them.

"Can we make it?" Bonnie gasped.

"We got to!"

They began to run, C. W. leading Blanche, Clyde helping Buck.

In the woods, someone understood, saw what was happening, pointed excitedly. "They mustn't use the car!" he cried. "Blast it! Cut it down! Don't let them escape again!"

The shooting began again, slugs tearing into the beautiful machine with devastating force. Paint flecked away in violent chips. A tire collapsed. A headlight shattered. The windows broke into shards. The body was riddled. The machine began to fall apart. Piece by piece. A willful and efficient execution, painful even to some of the executioners, and some of them stopped shooting. A bullet penetrated the gas tank, and another. With a rush of air, the doomed machine disappeared in a roaring wall of orange flame. The shooting stopped. The car died.

In the center of the field, not far from where they had spent the night, Blanche and Buck took cover behind a fallen log, unable to go on. Behind them, Clyde, Bonnie, and C. W. scrambled desperately for the edge of the woods, their last hope for escape.

Men began to appear out of the brush, to close in on Blanche and Buck, their weapons loaded and ready, taking no chances. They knew all about Buck Barrow. The men came closer, surrounding Blanche and Buck. Two of them grabbed Buck under the arms and heaved him erect.

"Don't!" Blanche screamed. "He's dyin'! Can't you see he's dyin'? Let him alone!"

Someone held her but she struggled free, stumbled to her husband, shoving his captors aside, lowering him gently. "Don't die, Daddy," she murmured. "Don't die. Don't die. Don't die."

The men took hold of her, dragged her away from Buck and others turned him onto his back, anxious to get a good look at the famous Buck Barrow.

"Let him alone!" she shrieked. "Let him die in peace! Let him die in peace!" she ended, sobbing weakly.

The officer holding Buck released him and he fell back and died. A low mournful cry came out of Blanche and she went limp in the hands of her captors.

Clyde, Bonnie, and C. W. made it into the woods. They kept moving. Bonnie felt as if her lungs would burst, and her legs were wobbly. But she refused to give in to the weakness. Any second she anticipated the police appearing in force, shooting them down. No one came.

They made it through the woods, across an open field, and into a stand of pine trees. Past that was a wide stream.

Clyde went in first, down the steep bank, waited to help Bonnie, slipping and sliding, into the water. C. W. jumped after them. They were halfway across, chest-deep in the stream, when the deputy sheriff appeared.

Without a word, he took aim and fired and Bonnie took the slug in the shoulder. It burned into her with a fierce intensity, and she fell over, screaming. Never before had she experienced severe physical pain and her cry was the cry of a frightened animal.

Clyde turned, spotted the peace officer, and shot. The man fell dead.

C. W. reached Bonnie first and dragged her the rest of the way. Once ashore, they made it into a cornfield, moving deeper among the stalks.

"Keep movin'," Clyde gasped.

"I got to rest," Bonnie said. "You go on without me ..."

They went on for a few more yards before stopping Clyde peered ahead.

"There's a farm ... gotta ... get a ... car ... got to. Wait here."

He staggered forward, working on pure adrenelin now, driven by forces never before utilized. As he came closer to the farmhouse, he spotted a car parked in the driveway. Unsteady, stumbling and falling, he made his way toward it, gun in hand, hoping with a rare desperation that no one would appear, that no one would try to stop him.

No one did. He struggled into the front seat and started the engine, turned the car back into the cornfield, cutting a swarth back to his friends. Nothing was going to stop him now. Nothing and no one.

He stopped alongside Bonnie and C. W. and got out. "Help me, C. W. Bonnie and me'll get into the back. You have to drive. Okay?"

C. W. chewed his lower lip. "Okay, Clyde."

"All right. Let's get out of here."

C. W., his normally placid face fixed with purpose, leaned into the wheel as if willing the car to greater speed. He was bare-chested, dirty, eyes swollen from lack of sleep. Time had lost all meaning for him and he had no idea of how long he had been driving.

In the rear seat was Clyde Barrow, bleeding from that arm wound, drifting in and out of consciousness, a man seldom himself. Next to him sprawled Bonnie Parker, her shoulder bandaged, her face drained of color, sleeping fitfully.

Clyde came awake, trying to orient himself. He shoved himself erect and focused on the back of C. W.'s head. "C. W., where we at?"

"Don't know, exactly."

"What time is it?"

"Don't know. Don't know what day it is, either."

"Head out, C. W.," Clyde said, some of the old authority in his voice. "Find us a place where it's safe and we can rest."

C. W. arranged his mouth into a flat line. "I'm goin' home to my daddy's farm."

Clyde started to say something, thought better of it, and fell back on the seat. A moment later he was unconscious.

Dusk was coming on and the car rattled along the back road. C. W. was worried. Bonnie and Clyde both were in bad shape, running fevers and in need of doctoring. He mouthed a silent prayer that they would last until he was able to reach home.

That's when he spotted the Okie campsite alongside a small lake. Half a dozen Model-Ts and pickup trucks loaded down with household goods, parked near a campfire. A number of families sat around the fire while the women prepared the evening meal.

C. W. pumped the brake and turned into the camp. He stopped the car and got out. All the faces turned, the tired, weathered faces of people defeated by the past and with little hope for the future. They watched C. W. approach with no sign of friendliness.

C. W. tugged at his nose nervously. "Can y'all spare me a little water?"

For a moment, no response. With a self grunt, one man rose and dipped a cup of water out of a bucket. He picked his way forward, eyeing C. W. suspiciously, withholding the cup from his reaching hand.

"Who are you, boy?" the man drawled. There was no hostility in the question, only the proper concern of a man who aimed to take care of himself and his own.

"Name's Moss. C. W. Moss."

That seemed to satisfy the man. He extended the cup. C. W. gulped it down, too fast, and began to cough. He fought for breath, and drank some more.

The Okie leader went up to the car, circled it uncertainly, peering into the back seat. He stopped abruptly and his eyes widened.

"It's Bonnie Parker," he said, in a hushed, almost reverent tone, "and Clyde Barrow."

He held himself very still, staring, while the others shuffled up to see for themselves. Bonnie was sitting up, holding her injured shoulder, barely aware of the audience. A woman detached herself from the crowd, to return moments later with a bowl of soup, which she handed to C. W. He accepted it gratefully, sipped it down.

Seeing Clyde stirring, a man lit a cigarette and reached through the window, gingerly, tenderly, as if fearing to do further injury to the wounded man, placed it between his lips. It hung there smouldering, Clyde lacking strength enough to drag on it or remove it.

C. W. finished the soup and handed the empty bowl back to the woman, thanking her. He went back to the car started the engine.

The Okies, men, women, and children, stepped back. Clyde looked out at them. He managed an almost imperceptible nod of his head, the only gratitude he was able to express. The car rolled out onto the road and sped away.

A small boy pulled at his father's pants leg. "Pa, who was they?"

"That was Bonnie and Clyde," he answered softly, "the bank robbers."

15

THE FARM wasn't much, the house, the barn, the toolshed, all ramshackle, just a few miles outside Arcadia, Louisiana. It was still now, at night, no lights showing anywhere.

The darkness presented no difficulty to C. W. He directed the car off the country highway onto the access road that sliced across his father's land with no trouble, negotiating the twists and turns as if he'd never been away, easing over the bumps, anxious not to jar Bonnie and Clyde. He drew up in front of the farmhouse and pressed down on his horn. A second time. He knew how heavily the old man slept.

A minute passed before the porch light came on, a dim yellow nimbus and a man appeared, squinting into the night. He was a larger, older edition of C. W., stocky and going to fat, a gray halo flaring off his bald plate.

"Who's there?" he challenged, his voice cold but uncertain. "Who's out there?"

"Daddy?" C. W. called.

Ivan Moss moved to the edge of the porch. "Who's there? Who is it?"

C. W. got out of the car, the night air chilly against his bare chest. "It's C. W. It's Clarence."

"Clarence!"

He picked his way down the steps and trundled toward his son. They fell into each other's arms and Ivan pounded his son's back. He stepped back.

"God, boy, it's good to see you, to have you back home. I can use you, boy, to help me work the land." A scowl twisted his broad face he saw something by the light of the porch.

"What the hell is that on your chest?" he ripped out.

"Huh?"

Ivan pointed. "That ... that *picture*. What the hell is that supposed to be, boy?" There was no ignoring the disgust in Ivan's voice, the thin scorn.

C. W.'s mouth curled nervously and he pawed his chest. "This here is a tattoo, Pa. You know. I'll tell you about it later on. My friends in the car, they are hurt. Help me get 'em inside."

Ivan stared at his son briefly, then went over to the car. He studied Bonnie and Clyde in the back seat with concentrated interest. When he swung around, his flat face was drawn together in somber consideration.

"Jesus, son, what happened to them? You in trouble?"

"Yeah. That's Clyde Barrow and Bonnie Parker." Ivan's brow's rose, but he said nothing. C. W. went on, "We been shot up bad. Help me get 'em inside. We gotta help 'em."

Ivan hesitated. "You think it's so smart, bringin' 'em here? If the law should find out—"

"Where else could I go? There was noplace. Please, Pa. They're hurt bad."

Ivan grunted his assent. He dragged Clyde out of the car, supported him on wobbly legs up onto the porch. C. W. helped Bonnie. Under the light, Ivan glanced unhappily at his son. He swore.

"Why'd you get yourself marked up, C. W.? A tattoo! Now what in hell made you do a damn fool thing like that?"

C. W. ducked his head as if he'd been struck. "Aw, Pa."

"I asked you a question."

"C'mon, Pa." C. W. said very quietly. "Open the door. Let's get 'em inside."

There was nothing distinctive about the office of the sheriff in Dexter, Iowa. A plain room with an oak rolltop desk and a few hard chairs. One door led to the street and another opened on a row of cells. A locked rifle rack stood against the south wall and a framed certificate from the national organization of police chiefs hung on the wall behind the desk.

The sheriff was a big-bellied man with pouchy eyes and a complex of purple veins in his bulbous nose. He sat with booted feet up on his desk, a humorless, square-built deputy standing at his shoulder. They were reading a newspaper story about the gun battle with the Barrow gang, a story illustrated with photographs, including one of the dead Buck Barrow.

"Look here," the deputy said, pointing to one photograph. "I was in the bunch that took 'er. See here? Can you make me out? Here I am, see here, right behind Joe Boyd here."

"Sure enough, Billy. Is that your head there?"

"Mind if I keep that there photograph, Sheriff?"

"No, I don't mind, Billy?"

He handed the paper to the younger man and watched while he carefully cut it out of the paper, folded it neatly into eighths and slipped it into his wallet.

"Still can't figure how we let them other two get away," Billy complained.

The sheriff nodded genially. "That Clyde Barrow, he's really somethin'. Seems as how nobody can catch 'em somehow, him and Bonnie."

Billy's eyes seemed to glaze over, to turn in on himself. "Yeah," he muttered, almost resentfully. "Well, maybe this boy'll be the one to do it, this Hamer guy. Boy, if he can't pull it off, Sheriff, ain't nobody but the whole U.S. Army can do it."

"I reckon that's right. You hear now Hamer quit the Rangers on account of Texas got that woman governor. Said he wouldn't work under no woman."

"Well, that's right," Billy said. "I'd do the same thing, exactly. That man is all right. Say, how many they say he shot anyway in his day?"

"Sixty-five, they say."

"Son of a gun!"

The front door swung open and a tall man stepped into the office, a man dressed in plain khakis, a man with wintry eyes and a handlebar mustache. A man possessed of a kind of sinister frenzy beneath a veneer of studied calm. One big hand came to rest on the handle of the .45 riding low on his right hip and he studied the two lawmen with open condescension.

This was the same man the Barrow gang had captured and subjected to private and public humiliation, the same man they had left alone and handcuffed in the middle of a lake, the man who had sworn a silent oath to revenge himself on them and had dedicated himself to that ever since. There was law contempt on his face as he addressed the two men, though his voice was quietly controlled and polite.

"Excuse me, am I in the right place? Is this Sheriff Smoot?"

"That's right," the sheriff said. "I'm Smoot. What can I do for you?"

The tall man measured the sheriff and found him wanting. "I," he said softly, "am Frank Hamer . . ."

Ivan Moss moved down the path from his house to the RFD box alongside the road. His soiled blue shirt was pulled out of his belt, the sleeves rolled to the elbow, exposing brawny forearms, the trousers sagging. He walked, head down, as if lost in thought, and once he tossed a quick look back at his porch, where Clyde, Bonnie, and C. W. sat.

They were healing fast, he told himself, and would probably be moving on soon. Less than a week had passed since their arrival, but Bonnie and Clyde, still bandaged and weak, were fast shedding the effects of their wounds.

And they were different. There was a quality about them Ivan could never perceive, couldn't identify even now, a refined essence, as if each of them had pared away all that was unnecessary and burdensome in himself. Bonnie, her face without makeup of any kind, was thin, ascetic, with a quiet tranquillity. And Clyde, the tightness gone, as if in again coming close to the earth he had been replenished, fortified.

There was only one item in the mailbox, the local newspaper, a weekly. Ivan returned to his place on the porch before beginning to read it.

"Read out loud, Pa," C. W. said.

"Yeah," Clyde put in idly. "What do they say about us?"

"Here 'tis," Ivan said. " 'Barrow Gang Escapes Biggest Ambush.' "

Clyde laughed. "That's a pretty good headline."

Ivan grunted, continued to read. " 'They got away, says Sheriff P. Smoot.' "

"*Smoot!*" Clyde slapped his thigh in pure pleasure. "He sounds like a Smoot." He snatched the paper out of Ivan's hands. "Let's see that." A wide grin spread across his mouth. "Look here, Bonnie, front-page news! Listen—'No trace of Clyde and Bonnie and the third partner.' That's you, C. W., boy. 'Police in Iowa were dumbfounded at the seemingly impossible escape of the will-o'-the-wisp bandit Clyde Barrow and his companion, yellow-haired Bonnie Parker.' "

Bonnie touched her hair reflexively.

"Yeah," Clyde said sardonically. "We just took wing and flew away." A burst of laughter tore out of him, a rising sound, running the scale too swiftly. "See that, Bonnie? We're the front-page news!"

C. W. clapped his hands happily. "Hey, Pa, how you like havin' a couple o' big deals stayin' with you?"

Ivan toed the wooden boards beneath his feet and arranged a suppliant grin on his broad face. "Ain't that somethin' for me? Somethin' truly fantastic. Right."

That made Clyde feel good and he leaned back in his chair, manner expansive. "Well, now, Mr. Moss, you been real nice to us, and I tell you what, let us pay you forty dollars for your hospitality. What do you say?"

Ivan shook his round head emphatically. "No, sir. No. No. Don't want your money. Clyde Barrow. Just pleased as I can be to have your company. Yes, sir. Any friend of Clarence's is welcome here, now you know that."

Clyde accepted the compliment. "Have it your way." He turned back to the newspaper, began to read. " 'Police counted one victory in the capture of Blanche Barrow and the killing of Buck, the brother, who died while Clyde fled.' " All the joy drained out of Clyde's face and he came lurching to his feet, all coiled tension and frustration. His face drew down and his lips were thin. "Fled! What do they mean by that? I coudn't do nothin' about it, could I?"

"Sure, Clyde," Bonnie said, trying to soothe him. "It wasn't your fault, honey."

"The bastards! He was already dead! Buck was dead! They know that."

"Sure, Clyde. He was already gone."

"There was nothin' I could do!" he continued to rage. "Buck was my brother, my flesh and blood. I'd never gone off without him if'n he still had a chance."

"Take it easy, honey. No sense gettin' yourself all agitated over some fool newspaper story."

"Fled," Clyde muttered, looking out across the fields. "Fled . . . they know better . . ."

C. W. stood up and stretched. "Hey, Pa, let's have some lunch."

"Yeah," Ivan said reluctantly. He didn't want to miss

anything. "You folks like something to eat?"

"Not just now. Mr. Moss," Bonnie said.

"Well, that's okay," Ivan said. "Just say when you are ready to eat. Anything I got is yours, Miss Bonnie, anything you and Clyde want. Let's go, Clarence."

He went into the house, C. W. behind him. Ivan jerked around when they reached the kitchen and were out of ear-shot of the porch, his face livid and full of scorn.

"How could you let 'em do it to you?" he ripped out.

"Huh?" C. W. said uncomprehendingly.

The words exploded out of Ivan's mouth. "Put that damn tattoo on your chest boy!" He jabbed a finger at C. W. "What a goddammed fool thing to do!"

C. W. glanced down at his chest, at the elaborate design etched on his skin, blue and red hearts and flowers and birds and ribbons that Bonnie had helped him pick out in that tattoo parlor. It had seemed like a good idea at the time. Still did, he decided.

"I like it," he said defensively.

"Trash, boy. You look like trash, marked up that way. Plain cheap trash."

He flushed. "Bonnie says it looks good."

Ivan snorted. "Bonnie!" All his contempt and dislike went into that one word. "What does she know? She's cheap trash herself. And him, that Clyde. The both of them, look what they do to you, and you don't even get your name in the paper. Clyde and Bonnie, it says, sure enough. And did it say about you, what you did, that you were there even? No, sir. An unidentified man is all you are. Nothin'. You're good enough to help him and good enough to get ugly pictures put on your skin, but ain't good enough to get your name mentioned. Not one time."

"But, Pa—"

Ivan, making his voice throb with emotion, said, "I'm just glad your poor mama ain't alive to see that thing." He turned away in disgust.

C. W. made a face, glanced down at his exposed chest. "I don't see what's so bad about it."

On the porch, Clyde was sitting alongside Bonnie, staring intently at the newspaper, brow furrowed as if in deep contemplation. Bonnie felt a stab of concern for him.

"You feelin' better now, honey?" she asked.

"Yeah," he said distantly. "I'm all right." He studied the black headline. "Well, Bonnie. We made it, really made it. The front pages. I bet everybody in the whole country knows what we done."

"Yeah," she replied with brief enthusiasm, then: "But I sure am tired of robbin' banks."

"So am I," he said.

She studied him curiously. There had been a minimum of agreement in his voice. Even now he seemed withdrawn, his mind drifting off in some world of his own making.

"Clyde, what're you thinkin' about?"

Her voice drew him back and his eyes lit up, his face animated, that quicksilver smile turning his mouth. "I got an idea, Bonnie. A real good idea. Look here." He held out the paper and indicated a photograph at the bottom of the page. Bonnie saw the image of a stern old man with piercing eyes and white hair. "You know who that is, Bonnie? Do you?"

"Uh-uh."

Clyde leaned back. He enjoyed this, wanted to savor it, released the words one by one. "That there is Floyd W. Simmons, the feed and grain king, worth over a million dollars. Says here in the paper that he gets up at six o'clock every Sunday mornin' and plays golf. Out on that course near the Fort Worth cutoff, y'know. Now one of these mornin's when he gets out to the fifth hole, he's goin' to find a big black sedan just settin' out there, with us settin' in it . . ."

Bonnie laughed briefly. "You goin' to be his caddy?" Clyde looked at her calmly. "I'm goin' to be his kidnapper."

The meaning of his words penetrated slowly. She said nothing, holding herself very still. "That's crazy."

He overrode her objection. "Honey, it's easy as pie. We have us a house guest for a couple o' days and then walk away with maybe twenty-five thousand dollars. By the time the law gets movin', we'll be in ol' Mexico, pretty as you please."

"When you goin' to do it?"

"Soon as we get back our strength."

Bonnie stared down at the photograph of Floyd Simmons. "Well," she murmured, "he sure don't look like he'll be much fun to have around."

The room was white and bright, stripped down to essentials, a room no different than any other hospital room except for the heavy-wire-mesh inner door and the bars over the windows. Such devices didn't trouble Blanche Barrow. Except for the pungent smell of antiseptics, she would not have known that she was in a hospital. A turban of heavy white bandages covered her eyes and since the day she was injured she had been able to see nothing. She sat stiffly in a straight-backed chair, feet together under her, hands folded in her lap. A nurse sat in another chair behind her, but they seldom spoke.

Blanche gave no sign that she heard the lock click or the outer door open or the wire-mesh portal. Frank Hamer, tall and righteous in his khakis, entered the room and motioned for the nurse to leave. She obeyed. Only after the doors were closed did he pad silently to a position inches in back of Blanche. After a moment, she sensed his presence.

"Who . . . is it?" she stammered.

"Blanche Barrow," he said quietly.

It was as if some alien and devilish creature had entered her dark world. She half-rose out of her seat, sank back,

"What?" she said. "What do you want? Who is it? Nurse! I want the nurse!"

"The nurse isn't here. But you have nothing to be afraid of. I won't hurt you."

She sighed, slow, lingering, and her shoulders slumped wearily. Her head came forward.

"Your husband is dead," he said in a low monotone.

"I know."

"You're going to prison."

"I know."

"It could go easier with you, if you helped. Tell us what you know. Where's the rest of 'em? Clyde and Bonnie?"

"I don't know."

"Where's the rest of 'em?"

"I don't know. Honest, I don't know."

"How'd you get in with them?"

"I don't know. I didn't mean to. I really didn't. Buck said we was just goin' to visit, we wouldn't be doin' no robbin' and stealin', and then we went to Joplin and all of a sudden they started shootin'!" A hysterical element seeped into her voice and her head rose. "It was terrible, all that noise and the bullets smackin' into things. And we run off. God, I was so scared. And then it was run all the time. Run, run, run. And I wanted us to go, I begged to go, but Clyde and Bonnie and C. W.—"

Hamer leaned forward. "Tell me about C. W. C. W. who? His last name?"

"Moss," she said. "C. W. Moss."

Frank Hamer almost smiled as he went to the door.

16

Rain slanted down, inundating the land around Ivan Moss's farm. For three days it rained and Bonnie and Clyde grew bored with the house, bored with the company of Ivan and C. W., bored with themselves.

Clyde sat around staring into some point in distant space, seldom speaking; and Bonnie had found her old black-speckled notebook and spent most of her time scribbling in it.

"What're you writin'?" C. W. asked.

"Time'll tell," she answered enigmatically.

"Aw," C. W. said petulantly. "C'mon, tell us what it is."

Bonnie raised her head and stared at him. Saying nothing, she stalked out of the house onto the porch. Out of the low sky, grim and gray, the rain poured forth as if it would never stop. The old restlessness was on her, the sense of there being a place where life was better and more rewarding. Her eyes came to rest on the car in the driveway and she felt a deep urge to be on her way, speeding somewhere, somewhere new and full of promise.

She tucked the notebook under her blouse protectively and sprinted for the car, climbed in to the back seat. Drenched, and laughing happily, she wiped water off her face and pushed her hair back. There was an old army blanket on the floor and she wrapped herself in it, felt warm and safe, home, almost. She opened the notebook and began to read what she had written, occasionally entering a correction.

Ten minutes later the front door opened and Clyde dived in. Soaked and solemn, he was without anger. She watched him shake the rain away the way a dog would. He drew a box of ginger snaps out of his back pocket and offered them to her. She took one and chewed ruminatively.

"They're good," he said, eating one.

"Uh-uh."

"Want another?"

"No, thanks."

He studied the interior of the car. "Ain't much of a car, but it's kinda nice here inside, with it rainin' and all."

"We sure spent a lot of time inside cars and goin' nowhere."

He frowned ld turned away. His face lit up. "I was lookin' at a newspape tle while ago. They printed your picture, honey." He lea d forward and his eyes moved over her face. "You sure don't look the same no more."

It was true, Bonnie had noticed it too. There was a new fragility about her, as if all defenses had been stripped away. Tiny lines had appeared around her eyes and there was the beginning of a furrow at the corners of her mouth. The pale eyes were still and deep and she looked younger, clean, her skin washed clean of all makeup.

She went back to her notebook. Clyde could restrain his curiosity for only a few minutes.

"What you writin' this time?"

She entered a correction before looking up. "I'm writin' a poem about us Clyde," she said intensely. "I'm writin' *our* story, Clyde."

He straightened up, adjusted the arm in the sling, eyes glittering. A sudden flash of excitement and anticipation slithered through him. Their story. *His* story. A smile sliced across his mouth.

"Hey, Bonnie," he let out deliberately, anxious to appear casual and disinterested. Not succeeding. "That's somethin'. Let's hear it. Go on, now, read it."

"Let me do this line." She did so and looked at him. "Ain't finished yet. There's more to come, and I want to read it over a couple o' times and make what's wrong right, y'know."

"Sure," he said, dismissing her words. "Go on, now, read it to me."

She took a deep breath and began, "The Story of Bonnie and Clyde . . ." She glanced sidelong at him and he smiled a brief smile of encouragement. She went on,

> "You've heard the story of Jesse James—
> Oh how he lived and died.
> If you're still in need
> Of something to read
> Here's the story of Bonnie and Clyde.
>
> "Now Bonnie and Clyde are the Barrow Gang.
> I'm sure you all have read
> How they rob and steal
> And those who squeal
> Are usually found dying or dead.
>
> "They call them cold-hearted killers;
> They say they are heartless and mean;
> But I say this with pride,
> That I once knew Clyde
> When he was honest and upright and clean.
>
> "But the laws fooled around,
> Kept taking him down
> And locking him up in a cell,
> Till he said to me,
> 'I'll never be free,
> So I'll meet a few of them in hell!

"The road was so dimly lighted;
There were no highway signs to guide;
　　But they made up their minds
　　If all roads were blind,
They wouldn't give up till they died."

She stopped reading and lifted her face to him. It seemed
to her that a fine misty curtain had been lowered across his
eyes. A shudder went through him and he made a powerful
effort to refocus, to return to this place and this time.

"Go on," he said almost inaudibly. "Go on."

"That's it," she replied softly. "There ain't any more."

"It's the end? Just that way?"

"No. I got more to write."

"Then write it," he said quickly, commandingly. "Finish
it, Bonnie. And then you know what I'm goin' to do?"

She shook her head.

"I am goin' to mail it into the Law, the *Law*, Bonnie, so
they'll know the real truth. And it'll be printed in all the
newspapers. And the whole country'll know. Finish it soon,
honey. Soon . . ."

When the poem was done Clyde sent it to the police and
eventually it came into the hands of Frank Hamer. He sat at a
desk in the squad room of a police station and read it with
interest.

The road gets dimmer and dimmer;
Sometimes you can hardly see;
　　But it's fight man to man,
　　And do all you can,
For they know they can never be free.

Hamer tugged at his mustache. He intended to see to it
that they'd never be free. He'd dedicated his life to that
premise. He continued to read.

From heartbreak some people have suffered;
From weariness some people have died;
But take it all in all,
Our troubles are small,
Till we get like Bonnie and Clyde.

A uniformed policeman came over to Hamer. "Well, what do you think?"

Hamer tapped the manuscript with one strong finger. "Sure. Let the papers have it. Let everybody know about Clyde Barrow and Bonnie Parker. I want them to know." He paused. "I'll make that poem true one of these days . . ."

It was a sunny day when Clyde sprinted down to the RFD box for the newspaper. And there it was! Bonnie's poem. Printed in full on the front page with a special box to make it stand out. Clyde let out a triumphant yip that brought the others out of the house. He thrust the paper at Bonnie.

"Read it, honey, read it out loud."

She did, including the final stanzas.

"If they try to act like citizens
And rent them a nice little flat
About the third night
They're invited to fight
By a sub-gun's rat-tat-tat-tat.

"Someday they'll go down together;
They'll bury them side by side;
To a few it'll be grief—
To the law a relief—
But it's death for Bonnie and Clyde."

She finished and glanced up expectantly.

For a long moment there was only silence; then Clyde emitted a wild whoop of delight.

"*Damn!*" he bellowed. "That's me!"

His mouth gaped open and there was surprise and pleasure on his face and it was as if he was on the verge of a gargantuan laugh that refused to erupt. He slapped his hands together.

"That's *me!*" he chuckled. "In that poem!"

Bonnie giggled. There was no mistaking the genuineness of Clyde's response, more positive than she had dared to hope for.

A widening sense of accomplishment took hold of her.

"A sub-gun's rat-tat-tat-tat!" The laugh started down in his chest, a low cough, rising swiftly, filling his throat and breaking out with tremendous force, unable to be contained. He laughed and laughed and the tears ran down his cheeks. "Right in the paper! All about me!"

Bonnie was laughing also now, a release, her body immersed in a soft joy that warmed and provided a new sort of pleasure, meaningful, lasting.

"Jesse James!" Clyde roared gleefully. "You hear 'bout ol' Jesse, now you goin' to hear 'bout Clyde. Clyde Barrow! Clyde Barrow!"

He whirled around as if dancing with an imaginary partner, breath gushing out of him in a succession of explosive puffs. He grabbed Bonnie and lifted her off her feet, swung her around. "Damn, Bonnie. Damn! You must've been one hell of a waitress!"

He set her down and laughed when she wiped away her tears. He bounced away and back again, a loose-limbed young animal full of the life in his veins and unable to express it fully.

"Ooooh, that Clyde! That's my boy, that Clyde!"

Again his arms went out to surround and embrace her, to swing her about. "Bonnie . . . The Poem of Bonnie and Clyde! Ooooh!"

"The *Story*," she corrected.

"The *Story* of Bonnie and Clyde! Oh, child, you really did tell that story. You really did it this time. Ain't you somethin'? Somethin' rare and special."

He pulled her close and his mouth came down to hers and in that halved second before their lips touched a great wild burst of triumphant sound tore out of him. Then, still laughing, they kissed, bodies straining against each other, mouths desperate, seeking, animal sounds back in their throats mingling with laughter.

They, almost didn't make it back to their room.

At precisely that same time, in Arcadia, Ivan Moss sat down at one of those small marble-topped tables in Eva's Ice Cream Parlor, his back to the street. He didn't look up as the tall man approached, settled into the wire chair opposite.

"You're Ivan Moss," Frank Hamer said softly.

"Yes, sir."

"I'm goin' to tell you what I want done," Hamer said, voice flat, demanding. "And you are goin' to get it done."

"There's my boy, Clarence, C. W. I won't have nothin' happenin' to him."

"That was our agreement. It's the other two I want. It's up to you to keep your son out of it."

Ivan nodded. "I can do that, I reckon."

"All right. Now here's what you're goin' to do." He pulled his chair closer and began to talk, low, intense, a kind of repressed desperation in his expression.

That night, after supper, they were all seated around the living room, listening to the night sounds of the farm.

"Clyde," Bonnie said.

"Huh?"

"Tomorrow, let's go into town tomorrow. I want to get some pretty things in town tomorrow. There just ain't anythin' pretty to look at in this house, if you don't mind my sayin' so, Mr. Moss."

"Reckon you're right, Miss Bonnie," he said, averting his eyes. "This place could use a woman's touch."

"Okay, hon," Clyde said, then: "You can buy an awful lot of pretty things in ol' Mexico if you got twenty-five thousand dollars in your pocket."

Bonnie stood up. "Think I'll be goin' to bed now. 'Night all."

Clyde rose and followed her.

C. W. rose and stretched. "Me, too. I'm tired."

His father eyed him speculatively. "Stay and talk to your ol' daddy for a spell," he said tightly.

"I'm sleepy, Pa."

Ivan looked up the stairs, called after Bonnie and Clyde. "Sure appreciate it if you'd pick me up some light bulbs tomorrow. Some sixty-watters. Three of 'em burned out on me this week."

"Sure thing, Mr. Moss," Clyde said. He and Bonnie went into their room and closed the door behind them.

Ivan swung back to C. W., his face flushed and angry. "Boy," he spat out, "they expect you to go downtown with them tomorrow?"

"Sure," C. W. said. "I always go with 'em. Don't you want me to go along, Pa?"

Ivan's heavy hand lashed out and caught C. W. on the side of the face. " 'Course I want you to go with 'em. You go with 'em. Only when they get back in the car to come home, *don't get in the car with 'em.*"

"Why, Pa?"

Ivan's hand swung again. C. W. held his tingling cheek. "Damn dumb boy! You listen to me, hear?"

"Sure, Pa. What is it you want?"

"You ain't to come back with them tomorrow. You make sure you don't hear? You leave off buying those light bulbs till the last and then you disappear. Understand?"

"Sure. But—"

Ivan hit him again. "There ain't no buts. Just don't get back in that car."

"Why, Pa?"

"I'm tellin' you for your own good." His voice dropped confidentially. "And don't you let on to them, hear?"

"Sure, Pa. Sure."

Neither of them could sleep. They lay apart in the big double bed, staring into the blackness, aware of each other but careful not to touch. It was Clyde who finally broke the awkward silence.

"Bonnie?"

"Huh?"

"You awake?"

"Yeah."

He sucked in air. "Bonnie." The words gushed out quickly. "Bonnie will you marry me?"

Her eyes swung toward him and she could barely make out his profile in the night.

"You don't have to marry me, Clyde," she said softly.

He grunted. "I know that. I asked you if you'd marry me."

She looked straight up at the unseen ceiling, making her voice formal, a false formality that gave no hint of what she was feeling.

"How could I do that, Clyde?" she said. "You know it's just impossible. We'd have to go to a justice of the peace and a justice of the peace is a lawman. We couldn't even take out a license."

Clyde rolled to face her. He chuckled quietly. "Hey, now, you sound like you been givin' it some thought on your own."

"Oh, no," Bonnie said, struggling to muffle the emotion she felt. "Oh, I never gave it thought. I haven't thought about it at least ten times a day, I haven't thought about it every minute of my life since I met you."

Her voice cracked and her eyes flooded. She flung herself across the bed, burying her face against Clyde's chest, her knees drawn up, her body racked with sobs.

Clyde wasn't sure what he was supposed to do. "Hey, Bonnie . . . what're you doin'? Are you cryin', honey?"

She fought for control and at last the tears stopped and there was only an occasional sob. "Clyde, why do you want to marry me?"

He made his voice light. "To make an honest woman out of you."

She understood his feelings without the words. Her mind turned over, reaching into the past before flinging itself ahead into the future.

"Clyde," she said, "what would you do, what would you do if some miracle happened and we could walk out tomorrow mornin' and start all over again, clean, with no record, with nobody after us?"

It was an interesting idea and he gave it some thought. The possibilities were endless.

"Well," he said finally, "I guess I'd do it all different. First off, I wouldn't live in the same state where we pull our jobs. We'd live in one state and stay clean there, and when we wanted to take a bank, we'd go to another state . . . and . . ." He broke off. The quality of the silence had been radically altered and he knew at once that he could not have said anything worse, that this was not even close to the answer she had hoped to hear. A worried note came into his voice. "Bonnie . . . please, Bonnie . . . hey, Bonnie," he ended pleadingly.

She did not answer.

17

MORNINGS IN Arcadia were the quiet time. Little traffic was in the streets and there were few customers in the stores lining those streets. So it was that Bonnie and Clyde were able to make their purchases rapidly. They made their way back to the car, arranging the bags and boxes in the back seat.

"What's happened to C. W.?" Clyde said, looking around.

"He stopped off in that hardware store," Bonnie offered. "To get those light bulbs for his daddy."

Clyde grunted and took his place behind the wheel. Bonnie came around the other side and sat next to him.

"Boy," he complained lightly. "My feet sure are hot." He took off his shoes and massaged his toes.

Bonnie giggled. "You plannin' to drive with your shoes off?"

"Sure, why not?"

He reached for his sunglasses. With an exaggerated flourish, he went to put them on and one of the lenses dropped out.

"Damn!" he said, retrieving it, dropping it into his shirt pocket. He arranged the one-lensed frame and made a funny face in Bonnie's direction.

She laughed. "You goin' to wear them that way?"

"Sure. Reckon I'll drive with only one eye open."

Bonnie shifted her position and rummaged around in the back seat, coming up with a little shepherdess made out of porcelain.

"Ain't that the prettiest thing, hon? Just look here, you can see every little fingernail on her hands."

"It's a pretty thing," Clyde said.

He switched on the radio and turned the dial. A country chorus was singing "Little Church in the Valley." He beat time on the steering wheel.

Bonnie put the shepherdess away. "How about a peach, hon? I sure could go for a peach right now."

She came up with a big ripe fruit and bit into it enthusiastically, juice dripping down the side of her mouth. "Mmmm. This is real good, Clyde. Sweet and juicy." She offered it to him. "Want some?"

He stopped drumming on the wheel. "Why'n't we do it tomorrow?" There was a bright, anticipatory glow in his eyes.

"Do what?"

"Tomorrow's Sunday, ain't it? We could drive all night and be on that golf course first thing in the morning."

"You sure you feel up to it?" she said after a thoughtful beat.

"Yeah. Why not?" His eyes darted up and down the quiet street. A car was approaching with no great urgency. "Where is that C. W.? What's holdin' that boy up? He's gone too long."

"He'll be along presently." She offered the peach again. "Take a bite, hon."

"No." He chewed his lower lip. "It's takin' too long. What if somethin' happened?"

"Nothin' happened."

The slow-moving car turned into the curb on the other side of the street.

"Go and look," Clyde said, suddenly irrascible. "See what's keepin' him."

Bonnie nodded, headed toward the hardware store. Clyde watched her for a moment, then turned away. His eyes came to rest on the two men getting out of the just-parked car. Deputies, both of them. Clyde jerked his head away, shielding his face with his hand. He pressed down on the horn, two short blasts. Bonnie looked back inquiringly. She saw the deputies and stiffened.

Clyde started the car, eased over to where she stood, opened the door. She got in and he drove carefully out of town.

"They ain't after us," he said, "but there's no sense askin' for trouble."

"What about C. W.?"

"Shoot! This is his hometown. He can handle himself just fine. When he doesn't see us, he'll come on back to the farm."

Neither of them spotted C. W., concealed in the dry-goods store, peering out through a curtained window, a troubled expression on his little round face, the tiny mouth pursed regretfully.

They were nearly halfway back to the farm, driving easily along a dirt road. An open field stretched to the right, a low green carpet of bean plants. On the left, a wall of thick, wooded greenery, the brush impenetrable. As they drove, Bonnie sang with quiet joy in tempo to the radio.

"What's that?"

She straightened up. Ahead a truck had pulled over onto the shoulder, and in the center of the road a farmer was waving for them to stop. Clyde pumped the brake.

"What's wrong?" Bonnie said.

"Don't know?"

A shudder of apprehension passed down Bonnie's spine. "Don't stop, Clyde."

He chuckled, "It's okay, sweetheart. That's C. W.'s daddy up there. His truck must've busted down and he needs a hand." He pulled across the ditch and stopped the car. He got out and strode toward Ivan Moss, hailing him.

"What's the trouble, Mr. Moss?" he called. "What's wrong with your truck?"

"Ain't sure," Ivan said uncertainly, eyes darting across the road.

Time slowed for Clyde. There was Ivan Moss, and seeing him made Clyde think of C. W. somewhere back in town, avoiding the ride back with them.

Avoiding . . . the . . . ride . . . back.

And over Ivan's shoulder, down the road, an old, rickety truck stacked high with chicken cages wobbling along deliberately, two farmers in the front seat. And Ivan, still looking expectantly into the lush greenery across the road.

Time stopped. Clyde backed off a step, and another. Something was wrong. Terribly wrong. He glanced around. Bonnie was back in the car, the door on the driver's side still open, inviting his return. At once he wanted very much to be back behind the wheel, speeding away from this place.

"I guess I could use a hand, Clyde," Ivan mumbled.

Clyde retreated further and time continued to hold. A breeze, icy, penetrating, made him shiver.

The leaves on the farside of the road rustled. Not from the breeze. And in that suspended moment Clyde knew, *knew*, for the leaves had moved unnaturally, in the wrong direction. He heaved himself around, movements clumsy and slow, and he heard his name spoken. A distant echo, the sound of doom, a voice long expected. But not so soon. Not so soon.

"Barrow!" Frank Hamer shouted, the signal earlier arranged. "Barrow!" the bitter tall man cried in cold rage.

Ivan Moss dived under his truck, scrambled for cover.

"Clyde!" Bonnie screamed sliding toward the open door, as if trying to reach him, to speed his return.

Time had stopped, and there was only the sound. Six automatic weapons spewing out an awful authority. Clyde staggered, stumbled toward the car, toward Bonnie, mouthing silent warnings and pleas, tumbling to the ground, body jerking and twisting, torn by slug after slug, destroyed.

And Bonnie, slender and beautiful, accepting each searing blow with feminine grace, body arching invitingly, white dress staining crimson, smashed back into the leather seat, falling finally onto her side, bent toward the earth, head hanging, hair a golden veil, an arm loosely and gracefully caressing the rich soil.

Dead. Both of them. Dead of eighty-seven lawful bullets.

Frank Hamer led the deputies out of the woods, guns smoking. He stood staring down at the two corpses, his face a blank, the far-sighted eyes glazed and lifeless.

Ivan Moss crawled out from under his truck, looking this way and that, seeking but finding nothing.

The chicken farmers had stopped their truck, now inched their way forward, horror imbedded in their faces. From afar, they saw the two bodies, shattered and still, and wondered silently what those two had done to deserve this. And knowing better than to ask, they returned to the truck, to the chickens. And drove off.

Time began again.

Two Coronet Books, from Hodder-Fawcett, that have been converted into films:

POINT BLANK
by
RICHARD STARK

Introducing Parker—the man with sea-green evil in his eyes and blood-black death in his hands.

There were six of them in the heist out on the coast. Three went down, then the other two crossed Parker up and ran off with the loot. That was stupid, for Parker could kill a man in seconds flat with his bare hands. From being hunted he became the Hunter. He cut his way through the syndicates, he beat his way past the gangland bosses. And finally—*point blank*—came the inevitable execution of a sentence that had been set the day the others got too smart.

LEE MARVIN stars with Angie Dickinson in the MGM film of the same title.

THE AMBUSHERS

by

DONALD HAMILTON

It was a damned strange cast. There was the shapely foreign agent, luring Helm into danger; a crazy guerilla General with an ex-Cuban Russian missile for a companion; and an equally crazy Nazi who couldn't forget that his side lost the war. All Helm had to go up against this bunch was a battle-scarred girl who couldn't stand being touched by men. At first, anyway.

DEAN MARTIN stars again as Matt Helm with Senta Berger in the Columbia film.